TEARS OF A WARRIOR

Stephen Paul Cooper

Printed and bound in Australia by BookPOD

A Catalogue-in-Publication is available from the National Library of Australia.

ISBN: 978-0-9924139-0-3

DEDICATED

to

Mrs Kelly

and to

Dolly Sprott

Part I - ….dream awake

Chapter 0

Innovation and design was his context, science and discovery his passion, but this young Haggis was more... much more, a *totally extraordinary* being. He was on the verge of achieving something more essential than good engineering and clever invention. There were few clues that some day, he would do something astonishing for the entire Haggii Nation, and their most formidable enemy too; humankind. If he can stay alive, maybe in time, he'll put it down to empathy.

Forget everything you think you know about Haggis or Haggii as they are known in the plural. Forget everything. Not just the bits you'd rather forget, or would like to remember... *EVERYTHING!*

I bet you think Tuna fish are small? Or that light travels in waves? Or... that Dolphins are clever, *eh?* Well, actually, Dolphins are clever but that's not the point. The point is this; everything you have been taught about haggii, you have read about haggii, *even* the stuff you've *heard-through-the-grapevine*, has been systematically developed, dreamt-up and disseminated to keep them down, undermine them, their nation, and their cause. Propaganda! The race of humans has oppressed them for millions of years, and finds it difficult to leave them alone to get on with their lives; an almost inbred need ifyoulike.

3

Many reasons have been expounded for this, some accurate, some not so accurate - reasons totally dependent on the standing, stance, and education of the particular historian attempting to explain this convoluted and delicate subject.

There were many bloody and cold wars between haggii and humans that lasted many centuries. Wars primarily about colonising and stealing the haggii nation's country and banishing them to the wastelands of Arctic.

You see, their homeland is rich with oil, coal, whisky, and due to the climate, millions of acres of arable farmland. Not to mention the diamonds and gold. The quintyllium speaks for itself. The land is very pretty - there are misty hills, mountains, and glens; constantly changing texture, feel, and smell as the sun arcs

the sky and the day journeys to its forgone conclusion. The light shimmers and changes constantly, bringing new radiant melancholy moods to everything.

Many crystal clear fresh water 'lochs' jumping with every species of fish you can name, and then some, adorn every Borough. Unlike the South, where massive overcrowding can make life unbearable, Alba is an unspoilt preserved and calm land; the best kept secret of the Nation. Or, is it? Every war is a tragedy, but every war fought between the Haggii and the humans is testimony to one indisputable immutable universal fact; envious eyes and jealous minds covet this wonderful land.

Chapter 1

Haggii - the Concise Oxford Dictionary tells us are shy timorous creatures that live in the highest and most inhospitable mountains of Alba, in the North. They are vegetarian, (mostly), and live very long lives, maybe a thousand years or more. Their favourite pastimes are writing and playing music, (mostly bagpipe based), telling unconvincing tales of derring-do and bravado, and frightening young Haggii with clever sleight of hand and cunning wizardry at their notorious celebrations and parties.

This is nonsense mostly, or at least inaccurate in the extreme, written by a human who has never been further north than the North-South divide of the Lowlands. Haggii are not shy, and certainly not timorous, the brave warriors of their Legions have proven this many times in the long and bloody wars with the humans and the Oraxonites. Nor are they vegetarian, although good Haggii always eat their veg. The music has moved on also over the years. The bagpipes are certainly loved by many Haggii, but ironically, the human-invented guitar is instrument of choice. Their parties and celebrations? More infamous than notorious really, but on this account, not too far off-the-mark.

A major point missed by our friends at the Oxford Dictionary is that there are two distinct haggii sects. On one hand there are the haggii that live by the Code, (never to be broken), and on the other Oraxonites, a faction that have turned their backs on this. The Oraxonites are against any joining of hearts and minds in a common cause, will stoop to any level to undermine and drive division between the Haggii, and are generally unpleasant. They have a particular dislike of human children and take great pleasure in ensuring agonising and bloody deaths for many of these in the most underhanded of ways. They are devout cowards, maybe the greatest of cowards, but have no illusions, they can and do hurt the most ferociously. This is a massive problem for the good haggii as the human rulers tar both sects with the same brush.

The Haggii Code comprises, essentially, four elements. The Wise Council of Haggii Elders decreed it in the distant past many millennia ago. In the beginning, there were many wars between the different haggii clans that made up the nation. At, or around this time, extinction lurked. The threat from humans grew stronger and became tangibly real, so, the leaders of each of the clans assembled in an attempt to unite the nation against their most formidable foe. They could no longer squabble over their petty differences, to survive they had to unite under one flag and fight as brothers. The Council was formed, and comprised of a leader from each of the clans and a deputy for each leader. Initially there were over two hundred members. The parliament building that housed the council was built and still stands today serving the same purpose and is a magnificently intimidating structure. Standing in the gentle autumn rain, it emanates a sense almost of... brooding. A shock of trepidation runs through you as you climb the marble steps and proceed through the humungous arthritic oak doors. For many centuries since the inception of the council, the membership was decided by means of birthright. That is, each member was there because his father was there – from father to son all these years, *legacy*. At a certain point in time and in a certain political climate, this was no longer acceptable; politically or socially, and there were many demonstrations and marches as to the justice of such an outdated and morally reprehensible concept. Think about it, would you trust a surgeon to operate on your vital organs if he had inherited his job? No education, no experience? Of course not. And so it came to pass, that to become a member you had to be voted in, or have served many years as a Scientist, Academician, or Engineer, and fruits of your work would have benefited the nation for a substantial period of time. The members that were voted in were known as the politicians, the members that were awarded seats were known as the philanthropists.

The leader today is Calculus Haggis, an engineer to trade, who has been a member of the council for over one hundred years and leader for the last ten. His narrow waist from all those years ago certainly hasn't changed places with his broad mind, but lets you know he enjoys the finer things in life. Very extrovert, (as engineers go), his suits are made from very bright tartans; canary yellows, blood-red crimsons, emerald greens, and electric blues. His ample mane is cropped and styled in a different fashion week-on-week and is a constant subject of wager amongst the younger members. Massively intelligent, he has an uncanny way of listening to all sides of a debate, distilling the salient points, and guiding the protagonists to a 'correct' conclusion. It's scary. Little does he know, the most important debate of his tenure is only weeks away.

Another modification that could be included in the dictionary is that haggii are meticulous about their diet and avoid over-indulgence or use of harmful foodstuffs. The top five bad foods, ever, as voted by the Nation, are - sugar, white bread, pastries, crisps, and caffeine. No self-respecting haggis would be seen dead touching any of these. All kinds of illnesses are contributed to their regular consumption – respiratory, digestive, and cognitive degeneration are exaggerated by the frequent intake of these foodstuffs. Also, the chance of developing cancer is increased exponentially. Not surprisingly, these are the most favoured foodstuffs of the Oraxonites. Not only have they shunned the Code, but they also eat products that are bad for their health and ensure premature ageing. All kinds of pre-packaged foods are full of these ingredients. Food standards have improved, packaging is very informative, but the Oraxonites cannot resist the taste of these. Even 'though everyone knows that vegetables, fruits, and unprocessed meats are good for health and well being.

There's more to being a respectable haggis 'though than just good nutrition. The famous historian, Prebble Haggis, has written many in-depth and eloquent dissertations on the Haggii nation's struggle and development over the millennia, including his famous thesis on the wars with the barbarians of Roma under the rule of the misled and insane emperor Caligula Caesar. The Romans too, desired Alba. A famous chapter is his rendition of the time that Hadrian Horatio Haggis spent many decades building a wall across the country to keep the Roman barbarians out. The only Earthling made structure that can be seen from outer space, bytheway. And it worked. A map of the world at that time showed the extent of the Roman Empire, covering around seventy-five percent of the world's landmass, and all of ancient Europe, excepting... Alba.

Prebble Haggis is a thin man, typical academician, bent over, stooping as he moves, eyes peer above half-rimmed spectacles, speaks with a cackley, breathless voice. He is very proud of the Nation and the Nation's heredity. A bit of an eccentric, often writes to the human Low-Lander's newspapers to object to the stereotyping, oppression and segregation of his fellow Haggii.

The wall still stands.

* * *

Shug was down at the Loch, again, paddling in the cool shallows. The water seemed clearer than usual, the glints from the ebbing sun hurting his blood-shot eyes even though he was wearing welderesque shades. He scooped up a handful of the crystal clear H_2O and flowed it down his hard-as-sandpaper throat

– ice cold, sweet, invigorating, 'too good to be true,' he thought as he submerged his head for a few seconds. Tossing back his abundant mane as he surfaced the torrent flung off spread in a large involutic arc soaking the poor soul who had sneaked up behind him.

'Awgghhh!'

Looking round he saw Hamish shaking himself furiously, attempting to come down from the surprise and vigorously striving to dry himself.

'What the hell are you trying to do?' he blurted and coughed through nostrils full of water.

'Hamish my old friend, what the hell are *you* trying to do?' replied Shug, trying unconvincingly not to laugh and failing miserably.

Hamish was Shug's best and oldest friend, a pal that took a lot of looking after, as he was always getting into trouble. Not *bad* trouble, as in illegal stuff or anything, but just getting himself in scrapes allthewhile. They had played together as fawns, had gone to school together in their formative years. But, as the years went by Hamish had fallen behind at school, and Shug had spent many hours with him going over the stuff the teachers were too lazy, or too old, to spend time on. Too busy spending time on the swots, easy fodder, getting their percentages up. Their friendship never suffered though, Shug taught as best he could, Hamish came on in leaps and bounds but would never be a shining star in anyone's book, excepting his mum's and Shug's, of course.

Hamish was big, a lot bigger that Shug, and was kind of unkempt. Unkempt in a clean way mind you, bathed regularly, but even the best kilts and sporrans were always a kind of awkward fit somehow. Endlessly, the Master Tailors were stupendously stumped. Having no teeth did not hinder his massive smile, which was more about the eyes than the mouth come to think of it. As a youth he got a lot of unkind stick about being slow and clumsy, but never while Shug was in earshot. Shug had had hundreds of scraps with Haggii that were too quick to bully and humiliate Hamish. Nowadays, thankfully, they're at a stage where no one dared say 'boo' to him or the consequences would be reaped.

'Sorry, Hamish, didn't see you there – what are you doing sneaking around like an Oraxonite on Safari?'
'I'm sorry too Shug, didn't mean to startle you – more to the point what're you doing?'
'Just watching the pelicans, thinking things through, you know?, the usual. Great fishers, aren't they, the pelicans? Quick, look at that big one, about to pounce.' And with that, the pelican in question's head dipped below the water and returned with the biggest salmon either of them had ever seen, probably heavier than the Pelican! 'Well, Hamish, there's a pelican whose family

won't be goin' hungry tonight. Anyway, what brings you down here?'

No Haggii on the planet would dare disturb Shug at dusk during his musings and attempts to make sense of the day. Only Hamish, who didn't quite understand the solitude required to put things in perspective, was cut some slack. It was fine.

'Well, if you must know - I've been wondering - you know the saying; 'hair of the dog… where does that come from?'

'You came all the way down here to ask me *that?* What's the matter with you?' Why would you think I'd know that?'

'If anyone knows - you will? Obvious, i'ntit?

'OK, leave it with me – another 'perplexing question' to be considered? – I'll let you know. Now, any chance of some peace round here?'

And with that, Hamish dragged a massive mitt through the water soaking Shug, and laughing in great guffaws as he galloped off.

Chapter 2

Why do baboons' bums glow in the dark? It was a profound question. A perplexing question. He couldn't get it out of his head. It wasn't the time to be drifting off in perplexing questions. He had to concentrate.

Things have improved between haggis and man over the last five hundred years or so, but some oppression is still there, and most segregation, but the haggii are now permitted to travel to many places across the lowlands and can seek work on a level par as the average human.

Who's Shug?

He's quiet, deep as the ocean, keeps himself to himself, and is kind to animals, including humans, looks after his friends, dependable, selfless, civil. He's an unlikely hero.

Much of his spare-time is spent contemplating perplexing questions paddling in the warm shallows of Loch Lomond, the biggest and freshest fresh water lake in Alba. The Loch isn't far from Shug's city and is surrounded on three sides by thoughtful snow peaked mountains, and on the other by rolling purple hills and planes dappled with the most exotic varieties of thistle, (a delicacy in all the best cafes and bistros).

He finds dusk to be the best time for contemplation and solving these perplexing questions, which incidentally is a most pleasant and rewarding preoccupation. Dusk he thinks, brings a certain tranquil serenity to everything, space and time and life-in-general. Or was that serene tranquillity? It didn't matter that much, he just knows it's a much needed diversion to get everything in perspective.

And today was no exception, the perplexing question troubling his weary mind this twilight was; "Why do baboons' bums glow in the dark?" Strange thought to have, admitted, but Shug had watched a documentary on Primates and there was no mention of it.

What could it be? Well, it's pretty dark in the jungle after sunset; could it be so that they can see what they're doing whilst making supper? Imagine all the baboon families each with their own little fires and frying pans cooking some tasty worms and spiders for supper. Their bums would light things up and they could see all the utensils? No, not very likely, the fires would light up the night anyway. Could it be some kind of mating thing? The brighter the bum the more capable the male is of foraging for nuts and berries? Is it only the male bums that glow? Shug paused to think for a minute. He wasn't sure that he could tell the difference between a male baboon and a female baboon. This is terrible - philistine! Should've paid more attention in anthropology classes. This should be the easiest perplexing question he's thought of for a while. 'C'mon, focus!' When the bums glow, they must give off a lot of heat, therefore, maybe it's to keep the campsite warm in the winter, a kind of replacement for under-floor-heating type thing? Unlikely to say the least.

Right, take it in small bite size chunks, one; they only glow in the dark, two; assume it's only the males that exhibit this phenomenon, three; the closer to the camp the brighter they become, four; they give off a lot of heat, five; 'hold on!' The closer to the camp the brighter they become? It has to be a way of navigating, surely? Everyone knows that the baby baboons are renowned for wandering off and getting lost in the jungle in the evening. This has to be the way they are rounded up and shown the way home just in time for supper. Getting some warmth in their bones is probably just a bonus.

Yess! Shug had it!

***

As everything began to fall apart in the weeks leading up to the stalemate, no one would have imagined the devastating impact that a young naive haggis would have on the outcome. Nobody would or could win, although, if the pain and suffering could be minimised, then the most optimistic optimist's dreams would be realised, and surprisingly enough, there were plenty of optimists. He couldn't have begun to imagine or define the wonderful creatures he would meet on the journey; Magdalena Magdolin – High Priestess of the Dolphins, widely renowned to be the most

17

beautiful creature on the planet. There's the Hezmanni ruled by the wise and temperate King Herod. A loyal and brave race, all of whom were ardent allies of the Haggii in many of the wars during the dark years, and still are. And, how about Sxsaxjsxjsx, (pronounced Sxxsaxxjsxxjsxx), of the Oraxonites, a nasty piece-of-work who preys on human children with razor like teeth, tearing flesh with a precision that mesmerises the watcher and astonishes the victim. His subjects call him Eric, an endearing nickname they tell him, but this is actually a coy ploy to avoid their vocal chords being shredded of an evening in his company through using his proper name. And, in no particular order; Doctor Daisy of the Xynbeme, the most faithful of faith healers, who will never ever give up and has let very few 'patients' slip through her hooves; Dani of the Icaria, a great warrior with a surprise or two up her sleeve; Sarah the fastest and canniest of the baby elephant racers; and Nathaniel of the Traxons, the greatest escort a haggis could wish for.

There are many more wonderful and exotic mammals, animals, amphibians, piscianians, microbes, marsupials, witches, bacteria, and rats, along the way, some good - some not so good – and some downright bad, but, they play their part regardless nevertheless.

Part II - If at First……

Chapter 3

"Not again!"

Good. Can't be looking too bad or she would have fainted again… surely? Shug's poor mum scared witless after his latest crash. She began to say something else as he fell onto his broken knees and the world came up to meet him… *lights-out*.

He surfaced in a queasily familiar sterile room, serious Haggii with brilliant-white coats looking over him. 'How do you feel?'

'My throat hurts.'

'Here, drink this.'

The Doctor supported Shug's head as he poured crystal clear loch water into his dry papery mouth. 'Not so quick Shug, a little at a time, easy, *easy.* '

Dr Jonathan Haggis. Shug had been under his care many times, in his numerous attempts to achieve the elusive ¾SofL round the mountain. That's three-quarters the speed of light to you and me, three-quarters of one hundred and eighty-six thousand miles a second. Even Sir Isaac Newton Haggis had begun to doubt the accuracy of his famous Laws of Motion equations at mind-blowing speeds in excess of this. The Jury, however, was out on the matter. Particle Accelerators were just returning to fashion and becoming sophisticated enough and tough enough to launch atoms to these speeds. Colliders were only marginally better.

The stoic Elders dismissed his quest as 'a waste of time and energy, young Haggis.' 'Haggii have no business travelling at these speeds,' they said unconvincingly in their condescending cackley voices, almost fearfully, as if trying to conceal something much more sinister.

Haggii have, amazingly enough, bio-speedometers in their anatomy that let them record very accurately the speed at which they are travelling, something to do with the position of the planets at any given microsecond. One hundred and twenty-eight thousand miles per second when he lost it this time. This was massively quicker than his nearest rival, Tiberius Haggis, who was also a good pal, (let's say they had a healthy 'competitive spirit' going-on between them). It was also a good bit quicker than his previous attempt several weeks earlier. It wasn't always like this though.

Another common misconception expounded by the Concise Oxford Dictionary of the haggii is that their right legs are shorter than their left legs. Shug was born, therefore, with a tragic deformity – all of his legs are the same length. Of course all haggii have legs the same length but the story has passed into legend and is exaggerated by the haggii themselves in a cheeky mischievous way to make fun of the lowlanders.

The Haggii Nation, having lived on the mountains of Alba for many Millennia, so the story goes, have developed different length legs that enable them to stay upright and travel very fast round the slopes of the mountain, but, only in a clockwise direction. This is because it is always the Haggis' right legs that are shorter, (another perplexing question that preoccupies Shug – why the right legs)?

And so it goes, the humans had attempted to catch and kill Haggii for many years, but were never quick enough to catch young Haggii, but were successful on a few rare occasions of catching older Haggii and ones that were ill. The meat of the Haggis is a delicacy, (regardless of age or viral content), in middle-class human circles. It was only recently, maybe in the last five hundred years that, the humans in a blinding light of awakening realised that if they chased the Haggii anti-clockwise round the mountain, with their shorter legs down hill, they would fall over and could be caught. This was disastrous for the Nation. It forced them underground, only the very brave daring to come to the surface of their beloved mountains on rare occasions to enjoy the ever-changing light of dusk and have the occasional race. It was less than a prefect existence.

Nobody these days, however, believes a word of it, (except the humans).

'...and that's not all, if you keep this ludicrous crusade up.......,' bellowed Dr Jonathan.

'Jon, Jon, *Jon!*' interjected Shug. He hated anyone who interrupted. Thought it was rude, so always interjected instead. There wasn't a Haggis this side of Hezmanomov that would get away with such insolence to the greatest of Physicians, and certainly none as young as Shug. Dr Jon was in the middle of yet another lecture on the perils of the Haggis' pursuit of the ultimate lap of the mountain. He couldn't help but smile inside, whilst outwardly putting-on a grim frown of disapproval, his young patient lying in such a poorly state and still having a go at establishment.

'...we've been through this a million times,' Shug continued, 'you of all Haggii know I can do it.'

'You can do it? Do what? Kill yourself and every young haggii to follow before you're a quarter-way through your lives?' His voice rose in both volume and pitch; 'bucking & weaving, and dodging & diving - daring, gambling, defying! Agreed, you are young super-fit athletes, aggressively confident and engendered with self-belief that knows no limits. You have a blatant disregard for your own safety and shrug off horrific injury along the way. You are adrenalised and stupid!'

'So, what's so wrong with that?, and anyhow those are some of my strongest assets, bytheway. So, in the name of all that's good and pure and right, why are you so against us... so against me?'

The young haggis was right, and Jon couldn't doubt it. He secretly hoped, and knew, that Shug would break the barrier. But he was a Doctor and a professional and had to be as firm as possible or his young friend may end-up paying the ultimate price.

'Listen-up! If you keep on with this crazy pursuit you're gonna' die. Have no illusions,' the good Doctor shouted as he turned and stormed off in a thunderous clicking of leather heels and whirlwind flurry of mane and clipboard. Just for ultimate effect of course, well anything less than bombastic would be a disappointment, wouldn't it?

It worked. 'Have no illusions?' This scared the bejezzus out of Shug, but wouldn't put him off. He had only broken half a dozen ribs, and both his arms, not to mention his patellas. And, skint his bum on the jaggy rocks, (which was easily sorer than all the broken bones put together), but *hey* he consoled himself unconvincingly; 'I'll be back on the mountain in six weeks.'

Chapter 4

One occasion, on seeing a photograph in one of the lowlander's newspapers showing a female haggis surrounded by many fawns, (baby, or child haggis), and entitled, 'a young haggis mother with her fawns,' Prebble Haggis wrote –

Sir,

Haggii have one fawn per year, other fawns in the picture belong to other haggii. Fawns like to congregate. Twins do occur, but rarely. Triplets are out of the question.

Yours…..

Sir? He has a certain dry humour that is wasted on the humans, but can't help himself, nevertheless.

Prebble Haggis is the greatest upholder and protector of the Code. He has done more, single handedly, to modernise and spread the word to every corner of the nation than anyone else since the forefathers who established it long ago in the ancient mists of time.

Any haggis that breaks the code is cast out and banished to the off-world moon of Oraxonos. Although they look very similar, you must never confuse an Oraxonite with a Haggis, and to do so would result in a noisy sweaty bloody death. Agonising! More on the Oraxonites later, what about the code?

There are four main elements of the code that the Haggii have lived and sworn by for over a million years, which are -

Courage, Temperance, Wisdom, and Justice.

Over the millennia many philosophers have proclaimed new virtues, or new lists of virtues, but in the end, regardless of what later thinkers thought, any list is merely an extension or plagiarism of the elements of the Haggii code.

Courage is a trait between the extremes of cowardice and foolhardiness. The emotion of fear is crucial to getting the balance right. This quality of spirit and fortitude is self-evident in all Haggii.

Temperance falls between the extremes of desire and abstinence. 'Everything in moderation,' as the great Benjamin Augustus Haggis was overly fond of saying. This element, it is often said, is the antithesis of gluttony.

Wisdom ensures a way forward and constant progression for the haggii, (regression is not an option). The Nation's crucial decisions are deftly planned and drawn-up by the deepest of thinkers, constructed and assembled by the most ingenious of

30

craftsmen, and established & implemented by the greatest of leaders. This is acknowledged and gratified by all haggii in family and working life.

Justice balances the haggis in relations with his fellow-haggis. Everyone is required to respect the rights of others, and this element ensures this. Every haggis is given his due. Clemency and mercy are closely aligned to Justice.

The plagiarists and band wagon jumpers came up with many pseudo virtues; *dignity, humility, modesty, continence, piety, compassion, affability, bravery, daring, spirit, munificence, fortitude, patience, and perseverance,* to name but a few, but these are all encompassed and inherent in the four elements of the Code.

The Code and the legal system were drawn up and the judiciary formed as the Haggii achieved stability after the many years of civil war between the different clans and tribes of the nation. And so it came to pass, the Council was formed and drew on the greatest minds and leaders of the entire Nation, the code was drawn-up and cast in stone. It has served the Haggii well over the years, and ensures a strong bond between all.

But the haggii aren't perfect, surprisingly enough, they do have a particular weakness; their love for spicy dishes, usually curry from the South Eastern continents. Shug's particular favourite is Vindaloo Escargot. This type of food is irresistible and, as everyone knows the dangers to the digestive system from such dishes takes his or her life in their own hands. Gladly.

Back to the Oraxonites – their favourite pastime is to kill human children by biting their heads clean off and swallowing in a single gulp. They are good at belching. This pastime ensures deep and chunderous belches can be sustained for hour-upon-hour. They are particularly underhanded in getting close enough to children to do this. Something along the lines of; they choose their victim and stakeout their house, learning the comings and goings of the entire family. The most common time for the Oraxonites to gain entry to the home is when the grownups are at work and the children at school, this is perfect for the cunning Oraxonite to gain access to the house and hide under the victim's bed.

They are very patient, waiting hours sometimes, until the child gets home from school has their supper and goes to bed, (after cleaning their teeth and having a good hot bath). If you think there is an Oraxonite under your bed on no account, NO ACCOUNT!!!!!, put your head over the side to look – whooommphhh, it's off in a single crunching of big jaggy teeth on young brittle bones, leaving entrails all over the bedroom walls for your poor mum to clean up. There are several clues as to whether or not one is under your bed. Clue #1 is heavy breathing almost wheezy and a pungent aroma that smells like your dad's old socks after he's been wearing his wellies all day. Clue #2 is your dog whimpering in the corner terrified that the Oraxonite will eat him, (the same reaction he has on fireworks night with all the noise). However, if your dog does this on fireworks night, can you be sure that it's because of the explosions, or because you have an Oraxonite under your bed? The best thing to do when you're sure they're there, is to lie perfectly still, pull the covers up to your chin, and go to sleep. You must sleep as this will enable the good

Haggii to locate the Oraxonite on their scanners and come to your rescue; they won't come if you're not asleep. In the morning you will not know they have been there, but the Oraxonite will have been killed, the mess cleaned up, and everything looking as if nothing has happened.

But, don't worry; it might never happen to you.

Chapter 5

Today was practice day and Shug had been in hospital a week when his thoughts turned to his friends and protagonists practicing for the next race, 'I hope nobody gets hurt.' All week thoughts of 'is it worth it?' scurried through his throbbing head. Excruciating pain and fathomless self-doubt were getting to him. 'Everyone knows the dangers, nobody is forced to compete,' he sighed, trying to convince himself to continue. And, what about Dr Jon? '…keep this up and your gonna die,' ringing in his ears.

'No, no way, I'm not a quitter.' He holds the ideal that in some places in the world there exists an intense intrepid love of high speed… and danger… a romantic paradigm. This has been engrained in his troubled mind always. The mountain is one of those places. He couldn't quit; it would be unfair to his friends to his family and to himself.

Tiberius was at the track and had just finished for the day when he found himself trackside watching the elephants practice. At the race meetings, the support race to the main event was the elephant race. This was always great entertainment, because, although the elephants were much slower, the sound was thunderous as four hundred elephants stampeded round the sturdy mountain; sixteen hundred feet hammering on razor sharp rocks, it was an amazing sound and sight.

But, due to the rocks being so sharp and the souls of the elephant's feet being so soft, special shoes had to be made to ensure they didn't hurt themselves, especially the baby elephants.

ArundleSprocketSphere was the Elephant Shoer. He designed, manufactured, and fitted the elephant shoes. Although he was doing a very noble and worthwhile job for the elephants, he was a nasty character. Darty eyes were set deep into a pointy chiselled face atop a small and skinny frame. Even for a rat, he had an unusually nasally squeaky voice, which was particularly annoying. Everything considered, and in the scheme of things, he was spectacularly ugly. He had a monopoly on elephant shoeing, and as such, charged the elephants exorbitant prices for their shoes which were very often poor quality. Because of this, many shoes sold bordered on dangerous even at the top speed of thirty miles an hour that the fastest elephants were capable of. It was massively unfair and made the haggii sick.

Also, ArundleSprocketSphere was an adviser to the government, the human government that is, (the Federation for Democratic Reform, or, FDR), and as a result conflicts of interest must surely exist? On the one hand he was providing a valuable service to the animal kingdom, and on the other was able to 'influence' various policies, including; level of taxation, land rights, inflation, and of course price of goods, and in particular… elephant shoes! The council of haggii elders had argued, unsuccessfully, for years that it was most inappropriate that ArundleSprocketSphere be in a position to advise the government on such issues. Unbeknown to the haggii at that time, he was also a major contributor to military policy and funding, which eventually, would come out in the wash.

The Hezmanni are a noble race and have been allies of the Haggii going back generations. Not unlike the humans in form, taller mostly, blonde and fair skinned, intelligent and measured and formidable foes to anyone that crosses or betrays them or, their friends for that matter. Their King is Herod, a good pal of Shugs on account that they had studied engineering at the same school at the same time and had never lost touch when they returned to their respective people and countries. Herod hadn't been King then, and was a lot of fun to be around – the consummate competitor in any sport or sparring. They stuck together in team sports, but on one-to-one competition they were more or less equally matched, Shug winning one competition and Herod the next. This has built lifelong bonds. Shug remembered some advice Herod had given him after a gruelling triathlon that he had won and Shug only managed fifth place; 'there's no point being upset or angry with yourself, life is special – don't worry about the times when you're behind – the race is long, and in the end you're only racing against yourself.'

They both excelled in the discus and the javelin and were very rarely beaten.

These days the pressure of ruling had taken its toll on Herod - the gaunt expression, eyes deeper set in his face bounded by dark rings showing that he neither ate enough nor slept enough; eyes that had seen one war too many. His muscle mass was vastly reduced from their school days too – skin and bone really. Shug had taken him aside on the subject of his health many times but was always palmed off with the almost mandatory 'I'm as fit as a fiddle, get out.' (Just how fit are fiddles, anyway? Another perplexing question)?

Herod had sent a message to Shug, saying that they urgently needed to speak regarding current affairs and rumour racing like wild fire across the land. 'If news had gotten as far as Hezmanomov, Jesus, it's bound to have travelled all the way past Argee, out to the Wastelands and beyond,' thought Shug. It went without saying that the Dolphins would already have a firm understanding of the crisis.

Shug and Hamish rose early for the journey to the rendezvous with Herod. As they set off, playfully nudging each other in-and-out of the puddle strewn gutters along the main street, the rain began to fall in a fine mist and got heavier and heavier and heavier, all the way to the outskirts of Haggii City Central, but as they crossed the City borders a prismatic rainbow shot skywards in a perfect arc, the torrent ebbed, and the brightening blue skies parted the desolate clouds leaving brilliant sunshine bombarding them with velvety ultraviolet rays.

Usually it would take about five days to reach the outer frontiers of Hezmanomov, at a leisurely pace, but with Hamish in tow and knowing there'd be some practical jokes and the obligatory meeting with Tom Foolery along the way, Shug budgeted a week. He also had a quiet word in Hamish's ear, 'Listen this is important. We need to be back for the race next weekend, it could decide the whole championship, we can still have fun on the journey to and from Hezmanomov, but we *need* to be back. Do you understand?'

'Yes Shug I understand, you don't need to go all melodramatic on me – back – next weekend – race – important - I understand - Okay!'

The well maintained roads of the City, surrounded by buildings and structures of glass, stainless steel, and neon, reduced to a single track and then to what was little more than a dirt track as they got further and further into the soul stirring wilderness. Shug loved it out here and galloped on ahead at a fair old pace leaving poor Hamish panting and wheezing in his wake. It was still early when he came across the small oasis he had discovered a few years earlier, which had a few dwelling places and a small Taverna selling local food and refreshments. In a constantly changing world, gladly enough, this place hadn't. Shug settled on the dewy grass out front and ordered food and refreshments for himself, and knowing it would be an hour or so before Hamish caught-up, decided to wait and get him something fresh at that time. By the time he did arrive however, Shug had had three mugs of the finest green tea – a herbal concoction from a secret recipe that would remain the secret of the Inn Keeper forever. Alchemy.

Suddenly, from behind some of the thickest leafed trees this side of Argee, appeared Hamish, galloping as if been chased by headless demons. Shug sprung to his feet and rushed towards him, 'What's up?'

'Here here, quick quick, take this,' bellowed Hamish.

Hamish held out his massive clenched fist as Shug extended his own – open with palm upwards.

'What is it? What's wrong Hamish?'

'What's wrong?' said Hamish cheekily – 'well nothing, have this.' He opened his hand dropping the biggest, greenest, stickiest rolled up bogie in the history of rolled up bogies that anyone had ever seen directly into Shugs outstretched hand. About five nanoseconds later, Shug had dropped the bogie like a hot brick and simultaneously dropped to his knees, vigorously scrubbing his hand on the still wet grass – 'you dirty bastard; it's like glue,' hollered Shug, 'I'll, I'll…' He couldn't finish his sentence. Hamish was galloping round and round in circles with his hands

40

in the air, doing some kind of obscure highland-jig laughing his head off – '*da, dada, dada*, got you… one up…. stupid Shug!'

Shug broke into a rueful grin; 'Grow up, why don't you? This is war – Sonny Jim, war I tell you, I'll get you back, shithead!'

It was at this point they noticed that a small crowd had gathered outside the Taverna, watching their harebrained antics, everyone wearing expressions that said – 'What in the name of all that is good and holy and kind are you two *doing?*'

Shug could hear, subconsciously of course, the inflection in the word *'doing'*.

'Taxi for the Haggii,' whispered Shug out the side of his mouth as he paid up, got some takeaway grub and juice for Hamish, and sheepishly left the Oasis. 'Thanks, Hamish – I'll never be able to show my face around here again,' he said, still chuckling inside.

They had to stay as far East as they could on the journey, travelling in a large anti-clockwise arc that would bring them through the foothills of Mount Ben Nevis, but more to the point would keep them away from St Icarus Bay and the Canyon of Fathomless Regret, two places you wouldn't wish on the completeist of complete Gits, (not that you know anyone like this, but they are around, believe me).

They made better time than expected, Hamish much calmer and enjoying many more of his 'clearer' moments than on previous trips, keeping the practical jokes to a minimum – nothing more than the odd soaking, hyperelastic bogie fight, or mud drenched wrestling on the slippery slopes of the inner reaches of Strathspey, the densest jungle in christendom, oh, and not to forget the evening he hid an ants' nest in Shug's sleeping bag. *That was funny!*

On the fourth day they came upon *the* mountain; Ben Nevis, the highest mountain in the world. As mountains go, it's a strange place, because regardless of the direction you made your approach, it was never until you were within about a mile or so of the base that you actually see it – a strange optical effect, brought on by the surrounding hills, forests, clouds, and rivers. The effect at first sight stays with you forever – the 'Ben Nevis' effect! Shug and Hamish still remember clearly the first time they saw it, yet today was equally as mesmerising. The first thousand-odd feet are covered in the most lush and rarest of flowers, plants, and shrubbery. After that, grey slate shoots skywards as far as the eye can see with veins of silver and gold squirrelly squirreling up the face – seams that are unmineable due to the density and sheerness of the rock, which was glistening in the morning rain. The two of them stood in a humble silence, absorbing the visual extravaganza in front of them.

'We've plenty of time', said Shug, 'do you fancy a climb?'
'What?' replied Hamish, in an 'are you insane' kind of way.
'C'mon, just for the hell of it.'

'We aren't exactly dressed or equipped to tackle the hardest climb on the planet known to man or beast now are we?' Hamish was being unusually clear and measured.

'Just the first thousand feet – what do you reckon?' pressed Shug

They looked at each other for a few seconds, both narrowing their eyes simultaneously, turning simultaneously, and setting off simultaneously at a super fast gallop arriving at the rock face a few moments later and without so much as a pause for rest or effect, began to scale the treacherous South Face.

Handholds aplenty ensured swift progress, until suddenly, Shug was in trouble. Reaching for a small shelf, it crumpled in his vice-like grip, which caused him to lose his footing and before you could say 'Arundlesprocketsphere', he was hanging at a very awkward angle-of-dangle from the cold hard rock; the only thing stopping him falling to a bone crunching blood curdling death three hundred feet below was the fact that his left hand was wedged in a small shallow crevice so tight it stopped the blood circulating to his fingers. Hamish saw the whole thing, and rushed sideways across the mountain to help. It wasn't easy, the plentiful handholds had depleted, leaving only voids and fissures in the rock to get a grip of, and even these were awkwardly spaced, ensuring high levels of stress were being experienced by both of them.

Hamish managed to ease himself into a position just below and close enough so that Shug could get one of his right legs onto his left shoulder. He pushed upwards so that Shug could just reach a handhold above him and to his right. As he recovered his left hand from the crevice he lost his footing again and slid a few feet regaining his grip just adjacent to Hamish, and in doing so ripped off a substantial patch of skin from his chest on the super-abrasive rock. Stinging!

They looked at each other before breaking into grins.

'Just for the hell of it?' enquired Hamish sarcastically.

'Let's get out of here.'

'Last one to the bottom's a sissy!'

* * *

Shug knew of a beautiful loch a few miles south of Hezmanomov that they could pitch up for the night and he could do some paddling, he was stressed out. It was getting late, the brilliant autumn sun just setting as they arrived on the bonny bonny banks of Loch Lollipop. Hamish knew Shug needed time on his own so had the good manners to make himself scarce on the pretence that he would forage for some food while Shug contemplated. They hadn't eaten since the morning. Hamish was rubbish at hunting but always had a go anyway. 'I'll see you in an hour or so,' he shouted over his shoulder as he headed off into the yellow leafed trees.

Shug plunged into the water and swam for about half an hour before spotting the secluded horseshoe shaped beach of iridescent red sand at the northern end. He swum to the edge and began to paddle and contemplate.

Shug thought of the Concise Oxford dictionary's portrayal, discussed earlier, of Haggis with shorter legs on one side of their body than the other, and being the oldest fallacy wrought against the nation, he thought it might pose a particularly confounding perplexing question – Haggii have shorter legs on the right side of their body than on the left? Let's begin - why the right legs? Maybe it was because the sun rose in the East? Everyone knows that Haggii have very sensitive eyes first thing in the morning, (probably due to massive consumption of ginger wine and whiskey on most evenings), so had spent many many years facing West in the morning with there back to the sun, resulting in their right legs being further up the mountain than the left and thus shortening? Not - very - likely thought Shug. Or, there wasn't enough blood in the body to permit the right leg to be full length, so by shortening this, the blood could circulate quicker? Again, not very convincing. Could it be that since the haggis has become the food of choice of the humans, especially at Christmas, they prefer to have a shorter leg to promote argument amongst human families as to who gets the longer leg, and thus spoil their party? Haggii would never wish anything but a fantastic time on anyone at a party, but on this occasion, being eaten and all, he would make an exception.

Yesss, Shug had it!

Part III – Abyss Staring

Chapter 6

A strange lot, a strange lot indeed, thought Shug. They would 'do' one another over for a Dollar. Betrayal came before loyalty, cowardice before heroism. Many were antagonistic and intolerant: Antagonistic *and* intolerant? That's borderline criminal! They can't all be that way? All humans? No, *no way*.

As a matter of fact, there were many that shared the same traits and values as the Haggii, the majority actually. Why, therefore, were they in such a mess? Disastrous economy cycling like a mighty pendulum on amphetamines, factions within factions, corrupt government, corruptible law agencies, and the corruptest military. Have famine where they need it, war when they need it. How did they arrive here, get to this point? Who got to the crossroads and decided 'yeah, this is the route to peace and fulfilment.' Another perplexing question?

Shug knew the humans better than most. He spent much of his time in the towns and cities of the Lowlands performing with his garage band, 'the Icarus Paradox'; it was the only way a haggis could mix with the humans - entertain them. Also, two of the band members, (drums and piano), were humans, which also helped. Haggii, when not being hunted on the mountains could in fact mix in this environment, but were segregated and treated as second-class citizens, regardless of how much they contributed to the economy, country, and world as a whole.

Made to give up their seats on the bus if a human wished to sit there. 'Encouraged' to sit in the backrooms of restaurants. There were even stories of Haggii being lynched by crazed mobs of humans who were quick to act but slow to understand. Haggii weren't permitted to vote, even 'though laws passed by the government affected them as much as they did the human.

Benjamin Augustus Haggis, a senior member of the

Central Senate of Nations, had campaigned tirelessly for equal rights for most of his adult life. He had had his home bombed, and been attacked twice by human fanatics; fanatical about being fanatical and fanatical about keeping a Haggii underclass, with the last attack putting him in Hospital for many months. Attitudes were beginning to change but there was still a mountain to climb.

The ruler of the humans was King Bob: King Bob the First, fondly known as Spitfire Bob. Shug was acquainted with him on account of his love of live music and, luckily or not, his insane affection for the Icarus Paradox. Bob seemed more open than the average human, had a quiet way about him and exuded an empathy with people, the animal kingdom, and life in general. This was rarely felt or seen in the lowlands, and as commodities go should be nourished with tender loving care. He was smaller than most, very thin, almost skeletal, had a trendy pointy beard & handlebar whiskers and an excellent taste in sunglasses, (round iridescent purple mirrors tonight). Lines of life covered his craggy face, knowing eyes shone bright. Shug had liked him immediately.

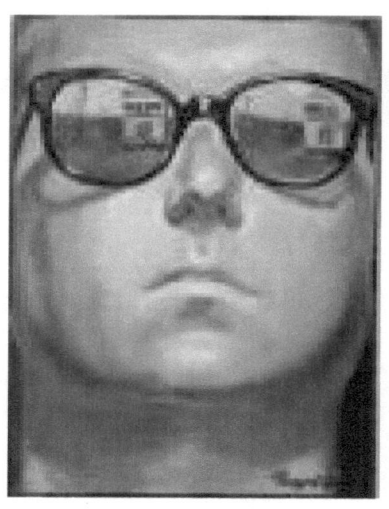

The same couldn't be said of Bob's right hand man, his Chief of Staff – Zax Vibex. Antagonistic and intolerant? This guy epitomises death and suffering. Enjoys killing to an extent that it is difficult to distinguish him from one of the lower order species of the animal kingdom, that is, the less developed of that kingdom not to be unkind to the average animal. Zechariah verse 15, paragraph 2-4: 'he who giveth forth and freely cold steel shall endure the Reaper's wrath for all eternity,' comes to mind. Revels in his tactile moments with his swords and daggers and has two forms of expression – rage and rage. Vibex is big. Much bigger than Bob. And wider. Lines adorn his face too, but these are not lines of life, experience, or education, but scars from the many wars he has raged against the Haggii and the Oraxonites. A black leather patch is nailed to his head covering the ocular cavity that once housed a steely grey eye. He kills with no remorse or pity, will never reach a diplomatic solution in any dispute, and promotes the segregation of the Haggii and many other specie to the detriment of the human culture and race. He is bigoted.

Shug pondered the relationship between intelligence and temperance, personified by Bob, *and*, stupidity and intemperance characterised by Vibex. It wasn't that Vibex was stupid, no, more…. underhanded – sly if you like. He could feel the embryo of one of his famous equations forming –

$$I \propto \left(\frac{1}{S^2} \right)$$

Intelligence, (I), varies as 1 over Slyness, (S), squared. *Eccellenti!*

There was only one main artery that was sturdy enough and sufficiently maintained to permit rapid travel between Haggii City Central and the Lowlands – the Low Road; the High Road, we'll think about later. Shug usually used this route because he was always late and needed to cover miles as quickly as possible.

53

The downside, well one of the downsides of this, was that he missed all the spectacular scenery between the Highlands and the Lowlands there was nothing on this route worthy of comment, very bland and barren. Another reason, the main reason he hated this road was that it took him very close to the main haggis' processing factory, which was situated near to the main gates on the Lowland's border. It disgusted him to think of all the law abiding upstanding Haggii who were only attempting to get on and lead a good and normal life only to be slaughtered and their carcasses brought here to be turned into foodstuffs for the humans.

The factory was as automated as automation can be – only a handful of human operators and maintenance personnel were needed to run this colossal operation that spanned around two hundred square miles. At the entrance to the factory were the mighty bays that the trucks would unload their sickening cargo of murdered Haggii onto large mechanical handling machines and conveyors to be transported to the wash facility that would, using the most high-powered of jets and chemicals, remove all hair from the bodies ready for the grotesque hide pullers that would peel them like an orange. Next were the bleed elevators that would bleed the cadaver dry and pack the blood in vast drums for use in downstream processes. Further down the production line were the threshing machines that would cut the body into sections; head, torso, arms, and legs. Nothing was wasted, not even the hair and skin removed earlier. The main muscle and flesh were sliced off of legs, arms, and torsos and these were the 'finer cuts' that the humans referred to in their delicatessens. Great vacuum pumps would then mechanically remove any other meat that still adhered to the bones to be jellified into a paste that was used to flavour their casseroles, curries and the like. Then the bones themselves were removed using side or quarter boning systems, crushed to a fine powder, packed in small containers and sold as an aphrodisiac. The spinal column was removed on the evisceration flight table to be used for the generation of stem cells that were used in the regeneration of nerves and tissue in humans who had a significant trauma such as a road accident. Shug couldn't even bring himself to think about the head conveyor or gut room. Intestines too, were mechanically removed for the production of pet food. It was disgusting. Finally the internal organs were compounded and compacted into the small three-dimensional obround shapes packaged in cellophane that is commonly known as haggis offal which is cooked with whiskey, potatoes, and 'nips for the humans to celebrate the life of one of the poorest poets in recorded history when compared with the great Haggii poets anyway, (to be fare 'though, he was one of the better human poets).

It gave Shug the dry retch just to think of it. Benjamin and Prebble Haggis had been campaigning for decades to have this barbarous activity outlawed. There were many humans who shunned the consumption of haggis and its by-products but there were still too many that 'enjoyed' the taste and in doing so provided an easy money making venture for the large Corporation that runs the factory.

But during the last few days, thankfully, Shug and Hamish had been travelling Northwards through the most spectacular scenery and landscapes anyone would behold. The route could never be taken for granted and the magnificence compounded the loathing of the Low Road. 'So, how was your journey?' asked Herod, 'or, do I really want to know?' Hamish launched into a discourse that could have lasted all afternoon if Shug hadn't interrupted – 'Can you get to the point? Herod's not here to listen to our inane shenanigans, let me tell a long story rapid – we left Haggii City Central, stopped in at my favourite Oasis, circumnavigated St Icarus Bay and the Canyon of Fathomless Regret, mud wrestled in Strathspey, had a swift skirmish with Ben Nevis, and arrived here safe and well!'

'What about the bogie fights and the ants-in-your-pants?' protested Hamish, palms up soulful eyes about to burst into tears if he wasn't allowed to finish his excessively embellished story.'

'How about, we head up to Herod's castle, we get our work done and tonight over a Shandy or two, you entertain all of us with your

tales of derring deeds on the hazardous journey here?' offered
Shug.

'And the mud wrestling too?'

'ObloodyK! And the mud wrestling *too.*'

Herod slapped Hamish on the back and put his arm around his
shoulder, 'C'mon young friend – wait to you see my castle and
my pals – we'll have a party in your honour tonight – Party for
Hamish, how's that?'

'Wow,' said Hamish, no one has ever had a party for me before.
What will I wear?'

'We'll worry about that when it's worth worrying about, but for
now; let's *get-it-on!*'

And with that, the three of them, shot off towards the castle
followed by Herod's sizeable entourage.

In the afternoon Shug brought Herod up-to-speed on the crisis
they were facing, whilst Hamish played hide-and-seek with the
Hezmanni children up and down the corridors of the castle and in
all the secret passageways, oblivious as ever.

'Let me understand. We have ten years' oxygen left and the
humans can see only one option – Mine the Quintylium from
within the Haggii' mountains to produce synthetic oxygen on a
scale large enough to save the planet...? Say it isn't so?'

Shug didn't answer. Herod continued; 'And your theory is that,
for years, the humans have been selling oxygen to other planets on

an industrial scale? You have proof to back this up of course, because if you don't you know you'd face the death penalty for sedition against your Crown, you know this?'

'It's not my Crown; remember… Haggii City Central is a colony.'

'What if the mining were to start – what are the casualty estimates?'

'Loss of the entire Nation in ninety days.'

A long pause followed, Herod trying to make some sense of the bombshell he had just received, trying to come to terms with the news. Until, finally showing all the gravitas he'd become infamous for, said; 'What are *you* going to do about it?'

'What am *I* going to do about it? *Well…* I'd like to remain optimistic that war isn't yet inevitable. Ben has alluded to an alternative solution, something to do with Magdolena Magdalene, Nessie, and the Edenite Collider, or something like that; he's being very cagey about the whole thing. He's meeting with FEPAC to canvas support and get them to try and see sense.'

'And the Elders?'

'They're talking about it. You know how they like to talk a bit?'

'Talking shops – all Mother Goose and blueberry pie, eh?'

'If I were King Bob,' continued Shug, 'I'd use the Oraxonites to do the fighting whilst using my own armies to protect the miners – less human casualties that way.'

'Astute! And what do you want me to do?'

'The Haggii armies can't be in two places at once, we can't fight two foes at the same time – if it comes to it, Herod, if we're on Oraxonos – can I count on the Hezmanni to fight for our homes and our lands?'

'Shug, this is everyone's fight, the humans through greed and sheer stupidity have jeopardised the lives of everyone – there isn't a Race across the land that wouldn't stand with the Haggii. I'll assemble my armies and march to Haggii City Central. We can be there in a week, and maybe, by showing solidarity and that we are indivisible comrades the humans will think twice about starting the mining. Is this what you wanted to hear?'

'As always, Herod, you're sublime! But, don't march yet, yes, be ready to go, but wait until Ben has zeroed-out all options – then my old friend, we will be decisive. Daily life in the Nation is continuing as normal as possible for now, everyone going about their business, all their hopes and aspirations on Ben's shoulders – there is a certain optimism that he can stop it happening.

'OK, we will await your instructions and be assured we *will* be decisive. Oh, and bytheway, less of the "old", you'll live longer young haggis! Hamish says you have a big race next weekend, let's forget the menace for now, enjoy ourselves tonight and you will be refreshed and ready for your journey back home. How does that sound?'

'Most sensible thing you've said all day!'

59

That night the Party for Hamish was as memorable for its raucous fun and bizarre games as it was for the veil of uncertainty that was at the back of everyone's mind.

It was a profound crisis.

Chapter 7

The qualifying had been disastrous, relatively speaking. This was the penultimate round of the championship, Shug trailing the leader by ten points, and he had only qualified on the second row of the grid. Leading the championship was Angus of the Clan from the furthest North – Clan Ork. He was a seasoned racer, had good race craft, excellent psychological skills and cunning enough to keep him at the top of his game in his fiftieth season. Shug on the other hand was in his first season, Tiberius his second. They were doing well to be running second and third in the championship considering the illustrious company they were in.

Shug was always a nervous wreck on the morning of a race, especially today; he had to finish in front of Angus. 'Nervous?' asked Tiberius. 'Just how much....' But before Shug could finish Tiberius chimed in with '*wee can you pee?*'
'Must be two gallons already and it's still two hours to the race.'
'Do you want to watch the elephant race, get your mind off it?' suggested Tiberius.
'OK. Always entertaining, lets go. Down to Benjamin's Dip?'
This was their favourite vantage point. Named after BAH from a terrible crash he had there in his youth. It is a spectacular right-

hander, blind apex, with massive elevation change – DOWNWARDS!

The elephants didn't race with the haggii, far too slow. As their top speed was just 30mph, the circuit was massively shortened from the 3 million mile long circuit the haggii had to compete on. Even at three million miles the fastest haggii lap was just 60.125 seconds. The elephants, however, raced over a three-mile stretch of the track, part of the terrestrial section, with the lap record held by Big Bill from BerriBerriHill, at just over two minutes and fifty seconds.

Big Bill is probably the biggest elephant in the world, a fair chance of being one of the oldest, and certainly the most modest. His eyes are as deep as the ocean, deep set in a noble grey furrowed brow, and for a beast his size has agility that never ceases to astound. His tactical skills are so good he can win a race before it has even started and has been winning since Shug and Tiberius were very young. His post race interviews are always short and to the point, almost blunt – doesn't like the limelight at all.

There was still a half hour before the race was due to start, so Shug and Tiberius wandered into the paddock area where everyone prepared for their respective races on the off-chance of saying hello to Big Bill. As always, the paddock was a hive of activity as many sweaty huffing and puffing creatures rushed to-

and-fro making last minute adjustments and devising solutions of cunning technical wizardry that would hopefully give them an edge in the races.

Half way down the wind-swept paddock they came upon Sarah, Big Bill's Daughter and Janice, Shug's young sister, tearing up and down the holding area practicing for their respective up-coming races. Janice, being a haggis, was much quicker than Sarah, but as they were good school chums and the fact that Sarah taught Janice as much as the teachers ever could, enjoyed spending the odd half-hour with her to get her pumped for the baby elephant race – a kind of role reversal when it came to racing.

'Hey you two – what are you doing?, you know the Marshals will exclude you if they catch you practicing here, and you'll wear yourselves out into-the-bargain, take it easy!'

'Wheeesht why don't you,' shouted Sarah, 'we're not *old* like you two!'

'*Steady.*'

'Yes, you're not too old to get a slap young haggette,' chipped in Tiberius.

Janice looked the part in her fluorescent pink quintyllium race boots that matched her body armour. Young Sarah too was looking good, very athletic and honed, must have been working hard on her training regime. Her skin had a satin texture that marked her out from the other baby elephants, lighter in colour too, not the usual battleship grey, but more a cross between grey and cream – a kind of autumn cumulus cloud colour. A bit of a scholar also if rumour is to be believed. All Shug knew was that he was pleased that his young sister has such a good companion in her group of friends. 'What would become of the two of them in these turbulent times?' flashed across his thoughts. They had been pals sine they were born and met up most weekends on Race Mountain. They stopped fooling around for a minute to come over and verbally abuse Tiberius and Shug, they knew of all the creatures in the land they could and would get away with it unashamedly taking advantage of their relationship. As always their banter was a mixture of undying support and acid wit put downs, which were always taken in the manner they were given – straight from the heart.

'Do you think you two can get in the top fifty today?' was Sarah's opener for ten in her husky squeaky voice.

'Yeah, maybe you won't get lapped and can salvage some family honour,' continued Janice.

Tiberius and Shug exchanged 'here-we-go-again' glances.

'You know we have never been out of the top ten in our careers and there isn't even fifty entrants in a race anyway, c'mon, do you want to get off our backs?'

'There's always a first time fat boy,'

'*You* can wheeesht, kido, how did your qualifying go?'

'I'm on the front row in my race.'

'So am I,' said Janice sticking her tongue through sucked in cheeks whilst furrowing her brow and cocking her pretty little head to one side.

The two of them were unlikely racers thought Shug, should be playing with dolls and making cakes at their age. Maybe he was getting old, times had moved on, youngsters these days wanted the danger and glamour and rush of racing. He was living in the past and smiled to himself thinking; about time I rushed headlong into the present!

'C'mon Tiberius, let's leave these hardened demigod racers to hone their inimitable and unsurpassed skills! See you later alligators.'

'We'll see you two in the recovery tent when they hook you up to iron lungs to get your breath back!' they shouted in unison as they galloped off to continue practicing in the holding paddock.

'They'll never learn,' whispered Tiberius.

'We never have,' sighed Shug.

As they approached Big Bill's truck, they saw him hunched on all fours, ArundleSprocketSphere working flat-out, hot smelly sweat lashing off him, fitting a new set of steel shoes to replace the set Bill had worn out in qualifying. Looking each other in the eye and without uttering a word, had the same devilish thought; 'we could have a bit of fun here,' meaning a bit of fun at ArundleSprocketSphere's expense.

'How's it going Bill?' An enormous neck of unparalleled girth lifted an even more enormous head. 'Oh, hi Shug, hi Tiberius… what's the word-on-the-street?'

'I wouldn't worry about the word on the street if I were you,' said Shug. 'No,' continued Tiberius, 'judging by the state of the shoes SprocketSphere's made for you, you wouldn't win the infants race today.'

At the same time Shug threw Bill a crafty wink. If there was anything that ArundleSprocketShpere feared it was Big Bill from BerriBerri Hill, his Nemesis ifyoulike.

'Yeah, they look like they've been chewed out of granite. Hey SprocketSphere, isn't it about time you sharpened your drill bits and cutting tools,' shouted Shug?

'And stop cutting corners on your materials, this stuff looks like boron steel!' added Tiberius.

'Oh…. eh…. ah…. finest quality…. great workmanship…. good price…' whined SprocketSphere in his usual broken dialect as he wheezed through noseless nostrils and began to tremble.

'Whaaaat!' roared Bill in his thunderous tones, 'let me see. If these aren't the best shoes you've ever made and fitted, you're a dead rat. I'll rip you in half with my mighty trunk and scatter your smelly entrails all over this town.'

'Wait, wait,' whimpered SprocketSphere, 'I am better quality shoes in truck, I get.'

And with that he scurried off towards his truck leaving Shug, Tiberius, and Big Bill in knots of laughter.

* * *

The human scientists had been observing the phenomenon for more than half a century, had been warning the politicians for a quarter of a century, had been calling wolf for a hundred and twenty-five years, and were just about to get serious. Benjamin Augustus Haggis was the only haggis member left on FEPAC, pronounced FEEPAK, (that's the Forum for the Engineering and Philosophic Advancement of Creatures). The Forum was founded when a need was identified to offer unbiased objective advice to the governments of the world on all forms and disciplines of technology, science, and engineering, that simple politicians wouldn't wish to, or could be expected to, understand.

In the beginning, only a few nations recognised the Forum as an authority for bringing to conclusion many issues that were the foundation of heated debate, intense argument, or frenzied war, but through the millennia all nations, without exception, have joined and abided by the decisions reached within its sanctified walls. In the early days the Forum existed only as an advisory board to whichever government required its advice, many of whom after lengthy consultation continued on their merry way regardless. As time passed and 'mistakes' were made, more and more leaders sought the advice of the forum and it wasn't long before no major decision on policy affecting a Nation's subjects could be made without the authorisation of the Forum. This was good for everyone, except obviously the politicians, as it meant it was extremely difficult for them to feather their own nests and acts of sleaze and shiftiness were easily detected.

As the Forum developed and matured, it became apparent that the philosophical aspects of life weren't catered for in any structured way and to 'get the balance right' this fissure had to be addressed. It had become biased towards finding absolute answers to every problem and every argument, and as life is never black and white, it was seen that absolutism was a hindrance to the peace and harmony sought by so many nations. And so it came to pass, its remit was widened to encompass the philosophical aspects of life as well as the sciences. Philosophers were elected to the forum, and added a much-needed new lease of life to an institution that had become jaded and 'too close to the trees'.

These days however, the Forum isn't the powerhouse it was then, and is seen by many as a talking shop of academicians bent on slowing everything down, dragging out and wringing the last ounce of blood from any debate, and procrastinating on simple dilemmas. Needless to say nothing could be farther from the truth.

The Forum assembled to assess papers, experiments, and the data acquired from hundreds of years of information gathering and sampling pole to pole and hopefully, would arrive at a plan to steer the governments from catastrophe.

All the data had a singular trend with one outcome assured unless the Forum could get consensus on their recommendations from all States across the globe, beginning with the Haggii nation. The discovery prompted the Chairman to address Ben directly.

'Ben, there is only one realistic implementable solution to this crisis, and it means the clearing of your Nation's lands for the mining to commence. I beg you to begin the evacuation of your people before the humans move in.'

Ben thought for a moment, silence fell over the Forum.

'Let me see, let me get this right. You want me to go back to the Council and ask them, nay; tell them that we are to abandon our lands? Pack up, up sticks, move on? Leave our homes our belongings; leave everything, because, and correct me if I'm wrong here, the humans through years of abuse and neglect have left the world with no oxygen and you expect us to make the ultimate sacrifice?'

The 'assured' outcome the scientists spoke of was the depletion of oxygen on a planetary scale that would end all organic life.

Already in the wastelands of the North thousands of creatures were dying every day. As a result, the microbes had migrated south into the Haggii Nation and disease had broken out across the land. The microbes being benign in the waste lands mutated and transformed due to the wet temperate climate they were now part of and had bred and caused the rise of killer viruses.

'You know it's not that simple, and the problem has been caused by all of us. No nation is guilt free'. The Chairman became sterner as he continued; 'anyone that stays will die, this is certain. The humans have mobilised an army and are transporting the mining hardware north as we speak. In a few weeks, work will commence and, for you and your people, it will be too late'.

Entirely out of character, Ben flew into a rage; 'You don't know what you're saying, you have no idea of the devotion and loyalty we have for Alba, no one will agree to move, war is certain. You can die from oxygen starvation or you can die by our sword, you stupid senseless fools, have you any idea what you have done here today, what you have accomplished?' Ben's roar reduced to a breathless whisper, 'quick to act, slow to understand.'

'It doesn't have to be this way. Ben, you are our only hope, you can convince the Central Senate of Nations that no creature has to die, that we can live together; there is a wealth of land to go around. It is a tragedy that your lands will be decimated, but you can go on, live and grow.'

All eyes were on Ben. What did they expect? What alternatives were available?

'There are options; mining isn't the only route. I'd like to think we have come further than this, are more technologically advanced *than this*. Resorting to mining? You know if we extract every last nugget of quintyllium it will only produce enough oxygen for, maybe, a hundred years. Then what? Abandon the world? Extinction? If mining begins, there *will* be blood. I shall return to the Council with your message and approach the CSN. Prepare yourselves.'

The five hundred year experiment had shown that, for many decades now, the oxygen supply of the planet was depleting. There were many reasons put forward as to why this was happening – ozone depletion, photosynthesis breakdown, bulk sales to other worlds, over population, etc, etc. Even conspiracy theories were emerging - the humans wanted the planet for themselves. Greed.

Ben knew the reason in its entirety and to a very significant degree of complexity.

Oxygen? Let's talk about oxygen.

As you know, Oxygen and its compounds play a key role in many of the important processes of life. Oxygen in the biosphere is essential in the processes of respiration and metabolism, (the means by which animals derive the energy needed to sustain life).

71

Also, oxygen was until recently, the most abundant element at the surface of the World. In combined form it is found in ores, rocks, and gemstones, as well as in all living organisms.

Colourless, odorless, tasteless.

Two of the greatest scientists of the first millennium share the credit for first isolating elemental oxygen: Joseph Priestley Haggis & Carl Wilhelm Scheele, a pharmacist and a chemist, both from the Eastern deserts.

Oxygen is formed by a number of nuclear processes that occur in stellar interiors like the sun, that is, deep within its searing molten mass. Are you still with me? In the terrestrial environment oxygen accounted for about half of the mass of the World's crust, eighty-nine percent of the mass of the oceans, and twenty-three percent of the mass of the atmosphere.

Several important ores are principally oxides of the desired metals, such as the important iron-bearing minerals hematite, magnetite, and limonite and the most important aluminum-bearing mineral, bauxite. Quintyllium is an oxide of Quinyttec, a massively unstable element which has, if legend is to be believed, certain mystical qualities. Eternal youth, healer of all ills, guardian angel, and, guaranteed wealth, are all attributed to the possession or wearing of Quintyllium. True or not? Make up your own mind.

* * *

Happiness turned to horror, elation to despair. The first corner, first lap melee of the baby elephant's race had savagely claimed a young life; Sarah. Big Bill was distraught, his only child meeting such a horrible, wasteful end. The race had gotten off to a good start after several delays due to the many crashes in the race before and a mix-up in grid positions by race direction, but as the field entered the first turn, Benjamin's Dip, all hell broke loose.

The race director put out a call for Shug to come to the medical centre. Bill was already there, several hapless medics looked upon the lifeless body of Sarah, everyone deathly silent. Many wept openly.

Shug wondered why he was beckoned, but before he could ask, a voice behind him said, 'Bill asked for you.' It was Dr Jon.

Shug stood silent. Wasn't good at this kind of thing, but instantaneously knew he needed to be here. Bill asked everyone to leave so that he may have a moment alone with his daughter.

Outside Dr Jon explained what had happened; 'A few of the calves got into the corner way too fast, too nervous - too inexperienced. Legs, trunks, tails, were tumbling everywhere, end over end over end. Sarah had had a good start and was in the top three but, unfortunately, was clipped from behind, sending her straight into the cold cruel blondestone of the mountain. It was horrible. Benjamin's Dip; dangerous dangerous corner, should be banned.'

After a brief pause Shug responded; 'Not sure Jon, ban racing? Where would that lead us, we're already living in a nanny state, the Governments taking an already unhealthy interest in just about everything we do. Ban it? We ban this and in the end we'd probably end up wrapping everyone in cotton wool. No one enters these races on a whim. We all know the dangers. But, is it worth it? Worth this?' Shug answered his own question, 'No, no way, not in a million years…'

Jon was surprised to hear this, knew Shug was the die-hardest of all the die-hard racers, totally and completely committed to the sport, so to listen to such a resounding reality *that is* racing was not at all expected.

'Never thought I'd hear you say that Shug, good on ya.'

'Do you think I'm not hurting?, after all, I *am* Sarah's God Father! Most of us come close to paying the ultimate price, but, do we quit, do we pack it in? And another thing…' his voice quietened to a whisper; 'I always thought that in some places of the world there exists a rich intrepid love of speed… and high risk… a romantic idea. She was a romantic. She'd want the racing to go on – so we go on, keep the spirit, keep the adrenalin, keep the purity.'

They were both traumaed-out. Grief replaced logic, insensitivity replaced sensibility. They had to hold it together for Big Bill. They stood in a numb silence for what seemed like an age, shuffling from side-to-side now and then, neither as in touch with his sensitive side as he should be, or wished to be.

'She looked peaceful, almost just asleep,' offered Shug finally.

'Imagine,' responded Jon, 'a gym bag full of the most delicate crystal dropped from a great height onto a concrete floor. She broke every bone in her body, every vital organ decelerated to pulp, she was dead before she stopped rolling.'

Bill emerged solemn, his sorrow sincere, his grief absolute. He approached the team of Doctors waiting to offer advice and console and do anything they could to ease his mind-numbing pain. Finally, in the gravelliest of gravelly voices he said 'Now, I will take her to our graveyard, thanks for all your efforts, she would have appreciated this.' He turned to Shug, 'will you accompany me on the way?'

This was a strange request, almost bizarre, and stunned everyone assembled into the softest silence. The Elephants Graveyard? On one hand the graveyard was thought to be fictitious, only a figment of older elephant's imaginations, who, beginning to question their mortality were attempting to find something that could keep their soul alive; a second life, transcendence maybe? On the other, however, it was a very real very sacred place, littered with sacred shrines and resplendent with hallowed planes, the only place a soul of the elephant species could rest in peace.

Shug was a believer and began to stammer almost incoherently; 'it's not allowed, only elephants, no one else, I'd be a tre…tre…trespasser?'

'You won't be able to accompany me on the entire journey, but will you please join me until I reach the outer frontiers?'

'Of course, anything, anything you wish.'

They set off immediately, last respects, wakes, and quiverings, were traditions not practiced by the dwellers of BerriBerriHill. Death is a difficult and devastating concept for any race, but for the elephants it is devastatingly destructive, many of who struggle to come to terms with the loss and thus become a danger to themselves. This was especially worrying, not just for Shug and Jon, but also for Bill's family too.

Bill returned to the triage lab and emerged moments later with Sarah draped rag-doll-like over his mighty trunk. Her tiny face had lost its angelic sheen and had taken on the mattest of Atlantic grey hues.

A cold flimsy rain had begun to fall as they set off Northeast towards Ben Nevis. They walked in silence as day became night and night became morning, Shug remained silent leaving Bill to fathom his thoughts and to try and make sense of what had happened. Word had travelled fast of the events that had unfolded the day before and many of the kindhearted souls of the animal kingdoms darted in and out the undergrowth, every now and then, to place flowers on their route.

Early on the third day, about a hundred miles ahead, a mountain came into view through the morning mist, a mountain that wasn't on any maps, in any geographical treatises, or captured in any aerial photography. At first Shug thought it a mirage, an image conjured by his overtired and fatigued mind, after all, he had been awake and on-the-go for three days. No, must be a figment of his imagination. Bill broke the silence. 'This is it.'

'This is what?'

'Our graveyard of course.'

Shug rubbed his sunseared eyes – 'amazing, thought it was a figment of my imagination.'

The mountain, or rather graveyard, jutted out of the plane rising vertically: A regal & divine presence. Marble white. Must be four or five thousand feet high. They were within a hundred miles, but why hadn't they seen it earlier?, – an edifice like this should be seen from a thousand miles away.

'To confess – in the last few years, I had lost my faith in its existence,' whispered Bill.

'How close can I come with you?'

'Don't know – I'm sure we'll be given a sign.'

As they closed to within fifty miles of the place – suddenly, at the base of the mountain a small cloud of dust rose into the air. The small cloud grew and grew until it was almost obscuring the mountain itself. It became audible too. A thunderous thunder of quintyllium shoed feet stampeding furiously across the dry cracked clay of the plane. A shiver of trepidation ran down Shug's spine. He shouldn't be here.

As the dust cloud got closer, they could just make out a massive elephant at the head of several hundred equally massive elephants – in a kind of chevron formation closing in on them at a tremendous speed. And, as strange as that seems, their colour too, was different - they weren't grey like other elephants, but more a white, or off-white – as if they were covered in a kind of powdery chalk dust. As they got within a mile of Shug and Bill, they slowed to a canter, and then to walking pace – until they finally pulled up about ten yards in front of them.

The leader, or whom they assumed to be leader spoke to them in a calming voice – 'Welcome, we are pleased to make your acquaintance, don't worry, we are with you now – come.' The elephant beckoned and Shug and Bill with Sarah, followed.
They arrived at the foot of the mountain, surrounded by the graveyard guardians. The same soothing voice commanded – 'give her to me.' Bill, at first, taken aback – realized that this was the moment they had came for, that now was the time to let go. Shug was overawed. The guardian extended his mighty trunk and Bill placed Sarah tenderly in the gentle curve. He then took ten

paces back and placed Sarah on the ground. The other elephants raised their trunks in the air and exalted an eardrum bursting symphony. All of a sudden gates in the rock, that hadn't been there before, or at least hadn't been noticed before – begun to slide apart in a grating scraping of rock on rock. Sarah stood up, Bill passed out and dropped like a mighty cooling tower being reduced to rubble by dynamite at the end of its useful life. He came-too almost instantaneously and looked on as the guardians placed a crown made from the most delicate of wild flowers on her head. She smiled a sweet smile before turning and walking through the gate, the guardians close behind. The leader beckoned – 'you stay here, you come with me.'

Bill nodded to Shug and followed the guardians into the mountain – deep into the mountain as it turned out. The massive stone gates ground as they came together in a resounding bang.

Shug waited. And waited. He hunched down onto his hunkers and waited, insecure and frightened, frightened for his friend. More time past and he began to worry; what had become of his big friend? Was he OK? Was he safe?

He should have gone with him? No. This was the elephant's graveyard – he had no right even being here. He waited some more. After what seemed like an eternity but was more like four or five hours, the massive rock gates shuddered as the mechanism that sealed and parted them burst into action cracking them open. The sound was still grating, but was most welcome. Bill emerged with the leader of the guardians. Some Haggii say that all elephants look the same – *no way* – Shug already could tell all elephants apart – and this one from the others especially.

In the same calming voice he said 'You,' gesturing to Shug, 'go back to Haggii City Central there is work to do and, Bill, return to BerriBerriHill, and don't look back on this place, neither of you – you know she is safe from harm now.' He turned abruptly and passed through the gates as they closed, this time, eerily quietly.

'Bill, what happened in there…, *Bill?*'
He didn't answer, he didn't need to answer, Shug could see it in his glazed over eyes, his gravitas graver than ever. Bill had seen the truth, had seen eternity – knew why we are here and where we are going from here, it was all there – in his eyes.

'You know, one of them said the strangest thing,' confided Bill. 'He spoke of you by name – said that you were going to need help, the help of many, and that the guardians would be there for you. He spoke of you by name!'

Shug shrugged. And, instantaneously felt stupid. Inadequate.

'We'll be there too, bytheway, the BerriBerriHill guys,' Bill continued, knowing Shug was trying to fathom the entire episode as they set off for home. Neither of them looked back.

Who would want to bark up the wrong tree? Why bark up a tree anyway?

If he can think of what kind of creatures live up trees, maybe he could determine the reasoning behind all the barking. Birds, quala bears, bats, snakes, butterflies, ladybirds, bears - sometimes. No, it was to disparate a group to be able to draw down any conclusions on the barking.

Does the saying mean 'Bark Up A Tree,' i.e. put new bark on the tree? Sometimes the tree surgeon gets confused about what tree he has to re-bark, hence, bark up the wrong tree. Massively thin hypothesis, and a bit stupid too. What about approaching it from a different angle? Who was doing the barking? It would be easy to assume that dogs were the barkers, no, too obvious. Humans are well known for barking, as in - 'barking mad'. Hmm… maybe. Bears can give out a frightful bark. Bears barking up trees at bears? Don't think so. Let's go back to the beginning; why would anyone or any beast bark up a tree? Is it a hunting thing? Humans struggle in their hunt for raccoons, as the raccoon is nocturnal only coming out at night. How would the humans find them? By scent? Sniffer dogs?

Raccoons? The raccoon has a lovely aroma and is hunted, killed, and mashed up, to make perfumes for rich urban wives.

Shug had a faint memory of a game the raccoons played on the humans. They would leave their scent at the base of a tree by rubbing themselves all around the bark to ensure the scent was strong, scurry up the tree to the highest branches, then deftly launch themselves through the air, maybe a hundred feet or more to a completely different tree. When the hunters arrived and let their sniffer dogs loose, they would immediately run and bark at the scented tree whilst the bemused raccoon watched from a completely different tree, hence; 'barking up the wrong tree'. Yesss, Shug had it!

Part IV – Segregation

Chapter 8

BOOM-DARRA-BOOM-SISS-**BOOM-WAH!** The last bar of the last song of the last encore. The crowd went mental. It had been a great gig, a cacophony of sharps and flats and what, with so many famous faces in the audience, WOW! The band hadn't missed a beat, cooking-on-the-gas as Annette liked to call it, which was all the more impressive seeing that the stage was so small you couldn't swing a cat on it. Spitfire Bob had asked to meet the band backstage. Honour indeed!

He wasn't comfortable with the adulation, Shug that is, made him kind of uneasy, the rest of the band on the other hand, bathed in it, (figuratively speaking of course). And why not?

The backing singers were the Haggettes. Three of the most beautiful haggis' in the land. They were also very fit, as singing is a very hard job, especially during a three hour set. Although Annette wasn't as fit as the other two, she still had the stamina to be as hot at the end of the set as she was at the start. A big lass, with rosy cheeks and massive smile, outrageous dresser, and not only on stage. Humungous earrings, white stilettos, short kilt, (green, vermilion, and blue tartan, sometimes), and shimmering emerald and purple and blue hair just to match. She could really fire-up an audience, and usually did. Her sassiness was legion.

It is not widely known, but haggii in fact have two vocal chords. The primary chord is used in every day speech and, for some, the only vocal chord they will ever use. The secondary is usually used when singing famous warloric songs of loss and bravado or reciting eloquent poems of undying love and being far far from home.

Annette used her primary chord in a gravelly way for the more grungy type rock songs, and with massive dexterity, harmonised with herself using the secondary chord to bring in a fifth harmony to great effect. How cool is that?, - harmonising with yourself without the use of electronic gadgetry!

The band had gotten into trouble in the early days for permitting the Haggettes to use their secondary vocal chord. Humankind had outlawed this practise centuries ago during the early wars. This was intended to put an end to the haunting ballads and euphoric anthems that the haggii used to rally their warriors in the days leading to battle. The law only drove the practise underground, and was still widely used by the more militant and patriotic that had never, and will never, forget their heritage.

The band had managed to convince the bar and club owners that were hosting the gigs, that the Haggettes were singing through Octavers, an electronic device that could take what you're singing and offset it, say a third or a fifth, or even an octave to get the desired harmony, and the funny thing is; they bought-it!

Enter Spitfire Bob. Rock & Roll bands do not curtsy.

It was awkward at first but Bob was more interested in shaking hands than waiting on ceremony. 'Wicked gig lads,' he said in an 'I-know-I'm-old-but-still-like-to-hang-out-with-you-dazzling-urbanites-now-and-again' kind of way. Looking around the dressing room he nodded to each of the Icarus Paradox in turn; Euan, rhythm guitarist rushed to shake his hand and welcome him to the inner sanctum with a resounding 'hello!' nearly ripping Bob's arm off at the shoulder in the process, the adrenalin of the gig still rushing through his veins. Macbeth, the Piper, waved a massive mitt in the air and threw a warm smile in Bob's general direction. On keyboards was John, a shy retiring academic who stood shoulders hunched in the corner staring at his feet not knowing whether to come or go. Mohawk, the drummer, grunted and the Haggettes, being satirical rather than polite, curtsied in beautifully precise unison. 'What's the progress Bob?,' said Annette in a forthright and confident kind of way, meaning, 'what are you doing about the segregation and beatings.' Bob was taken aback by this young haggis' affront and tenacity but not wrong footed. He had been around long enough and had the mud on his boots to know how to deflect a difficult question rather than give an incriminating answer. Vibex, in his usual slimy underhanded way changed the subject for him...

'You have a lovely voice, and I can't believe for a minute you'd stoop to electronic wizardry to get you through some of the more, shall we say, difficult vocal arrangements,' giving a slight clearing of his throat as he did so.

Swine! They knew he could withdraw their performing rights license in the wink of an eye, and have them disbarred from the Musicians Union equally as quick. In his singular mind, he thought; this would stop the awkward questions. He thought wrong.

'Will you guys ever see or understand the point', said Euan, 'I know the segregation and the oppression have diminished but the underlying premise is still evident, very real... if you want our help...'

'We've been through this a million times, interrupted Bob, but... it *will* be resolved, you have to be patient, trust me on this.'

'Patient?' *Patient?* You've been hunting us, stealing from us, oppressing us for over a thousand years. The advances made in the last decade are being eroded by *your* government and the military, especially You!'

'Shug, Shug... Shug. This is my right-hand-man, and one of the most loyal and honest people in my Kingdom. Zax Vibex is loved and revered universally amongst my people'.

'And has also murdered many of my people' protested Shug.

'They were killed in the wars, and you can hardly blame Vibex for doing his job, calling it murder doesn't help anyone,' objected Bob.

'Vibex is dangerous, his views are disastrous.'

Bob was never black and white like his ancestors, more light-and-shade if you like, astonishing for Royalty really. Also, he was on Shug's side, and Shug's Nation's side and not just because he needed the Nation more than ever, he genuinely had empathy for Shug and his people.

The Haggii had been hunted, killed, and eaten, for two million years, exactly the same length of time since the ape descendents had learned to use 'implements' to improve the efficiency of their hunting and thus greatly augment their diet. *Evolved!* But now it was getting dirty. In the same two million years, the Haggii had gotten quicker and quicker *and quicker*, now achieving near light speeds. No human had a chance of catching a haggis. Until recently that is.

The lowlander's awakening, discussed earlier, had prompted panic in the Nation and much debate amongst the Elders. Some lost the place and were expounding opinions like - 'time to fight', 'let's go to war,' 'time for action'. It was the easy option – annihilate the humans. This not only broke every decree of the code, but many ideals that were 'in-the-spirit' of the code.

Oxygen wasn't the only problem – the hunting and killing of haggii was still rife and tempers ran high.

'It can't be allowed', exploded Shug, 'we rise to arms and we're no better that them..., the same. Violence is a mental illness. It arises in minds that have been wounded in their capacity to build and sustain mammal empathy. The spiral of violence feeds on more violence, a vortex of barbarism, misery, and shame, dealt out by beings whose love lies shredded on the cobblestones. We must shift from violence to non-violence.' Ben listened impassively, silently impressed by his young friend's eloquence. 'We need to talk, continue negotiations. King Bob will back us – we just need to win over the government and the military. Hunting will be outlawed, the segregation will cease, oppression gone forever, we can live together, co-exist.'

'Noble and elegant words,' chimed in Tiberius, 'but with due respect, a little naïve. I can never trust them, they have never been trustworthy. We need to make a stand and make it now. They will never permit us to get on with our lives, we have been betrayed many times, many Haggii have died, and for what? As for Vibex he is a dangerous philistine who displays an alarming lack of empathy. You'll never win him over.'

Shug couldn't believe it. His best friend taking the side of the fanatics contradicting his views both their views, or so he thought. Obviously not. He and Tiberius had discussed the code many times, and the relevance of it, a million years after it had been decreed, but had always came to the same conclusion. They agreed the code was still relevant, very relevant; the world had changed, but was still worth fighting for. They had agreed!

And now this. Shug was about to let his anger get the better of him when he caught Ben's eye, or rather, Ben caught his; he looked to the floor and gave a slight shake of his head. Very subtle, almost indeterminable. Shug had spent enough time with him to understand that his gesturing said that it was better to back-off, discuss the matter in private and find the middle ground rather than have a row that could alienate many of the council, after all, Shug and Tiberius weren't even elected to the council, far too young. They were only present as advisers. Shug couldn't come to terms with the premise that a lack of a decision is also a decision. Didn't make sense, somehow, or did it?

Ben stood up. The rabble that had erupted as a result of Tiberius' bombshell died down and everyone waited what was expected to be the wisest words of the debate. The silence was cacophonic.

'Can you hear yourselves? I'm bitterly disappointed, but can't say surprised. The atmosphere of hatred against the human has grown heavier and heavier in recent times. They arrived in the days of our ancestors and our future grew uncertain, darkness entered our lives. We all know that what is happening is wrong.

So we take up arms? Another hundred years of pain, heartache, and bloodshed? - and what then? Does it have to be this way...? Too many of us talk without knowing really what we are talking about. Good information is essential in making correct decisions – both ethical and intellectual.'

He paused, seemed deflated, scunnered, before continuing; 'I suggest this; we will continue with the Siren Initiative. The Haggettes have all but eradicated the hunters. We will continue dialogue with the human. Remember, we are very close to an agreement, quintyllium and oxygen are the best bargaining tools we have ever had. If they agree to our terms, peace will be restored throughout the world for the first time in a thousand years. It is the better option, no, the only option to move forward. What do *you* think?' Reverberation ran around the Council. Ben had many allies, but also many enemies. There were those that thought he had influenced the council for too long and was becoming too liberal in his thinking. This was wildly untrue of course. Ben was as radical now as he had been when he was first elected, but was wiser and could see that no solution was obtainable through war. Civil disobedience helped and furthered the cause, but the ultimate goal could only be achieved by compromise: compromise on both sides. The Haggii could save the world, but the cost to the human was high, but not unreasonable. Treat us as equals. Leave our lands. Stop the killing. Stop the hunting.

Chapter 9

Now the Techie bit. *PAY ATTENTION!!!*

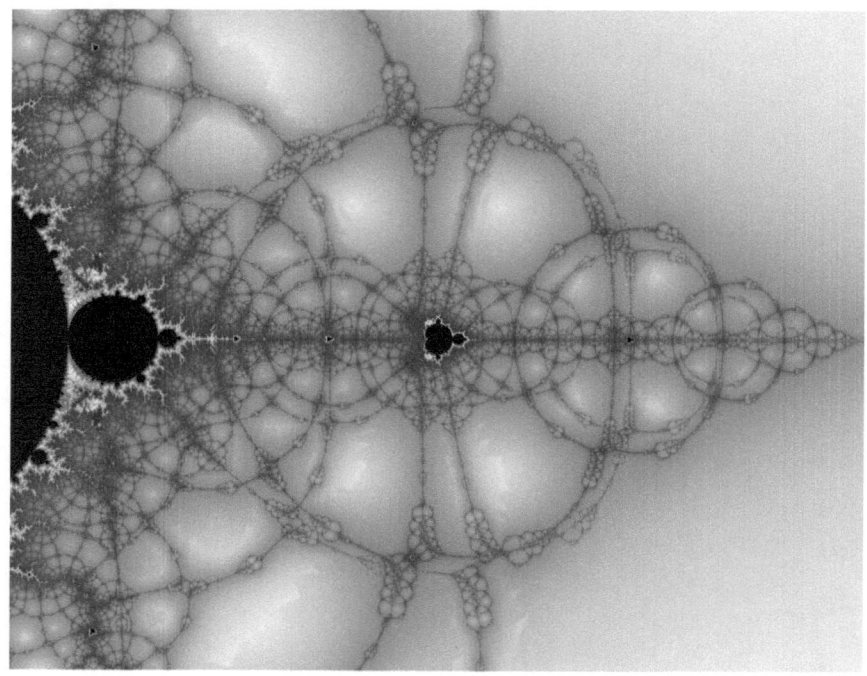

The chemical symbol for atomic oxygen is O, its atomic number is eight, and its atomic weight is sixteen. It makes up twenty-one % of the volume of the air we breathe. If it weren't for oxygen, life on our world would be very different to what it is today. Oxygen, the Elders tell us, is formed in hydrogen-burning stars, like our sun, by the capture of a proton by the isotopes of nitrogen and fluorine, with the subsequent emission of a gamma ray and an alpha particle. Helium-burning stars are a different kettle of fish altogether – so don't even go there.

Three naturally occurring isotopes of oxygen have been found: one with mass sixteen, which accounts for ninety-nine percent of all our oxygen, the other two find their major use in experiments for haggii scientists to follow the steps of chemical reactions. These rarer isotopes can be manufactured artificially, and *maybe*, in the quantities required to sustain life on our planet.

If oxygen at a pressure of one atmosphere is cooled, it will turn to liquid at minus one hundred and eighty-three degrees centigrade, which is very cold. You think snowmen get it rough? It's way colder than that. This, thought of another way is it's boiling point, which is a hard concept to grasp, but stay with me. You may already know that the liquid and solid forms of oxygen have a pale blue colour, which is caused by billions of tiny tiny microorganisms rushing around within the atoms at an atomic level. The critical temperature for oxygen, the temperature above which it is impossible to liquefy the gas, no matter how much pressure is applied, is minus one hundred and twenty degrees centigrade. Oxygen can exist in two states simultaneously – as a liquid and as a gas, but takes a pressure of fifty atmospheres. And we know that force is mass multiplied by acceleration and we also know that gravitational acceleration is nine point eight one metres per second per second, this means that fifty atmospheres is seven hundred pounds on every square inch of your body, this is like Big Bill from BerriBerriHill and all his pals sitting on you. Ouch!

Molecular oxygen can be converted to atomic oxygen by ultraviolet radiation at wavelengths less than one hundred and ninety-three nanometres, (this is very small, think of the distance between two coats of paint). Solar radiation striking stratospheric oxygen has this affect, incidentally. The atomic oxygen created in this fashion will react with molecular oxygen to form Ozone, which makes up our ever-depleting ozone layer, another headache for the Elders.

The oxidation of quintyllium is a very different process to that of metallic elements. For one – the oxide of most metals form very stable structures, the oxide of quintyllium is massively unstable.

As quintyllium is neither metal nor organism, the oxidation is a complex process involving impurities in the quintyllium, as well as water and carbon dioxide. Unlike metals, enzymes and impurities in the substance help these reactions and selectively control the oxidative destruction of quintyllium. Thus it is oxidized principally through the agency of microorganisms, put simply; *this element is metabolized by means of biological processes*. The effect is pronounced at elevated temperatures or within strong electromagnetic fields. This effect worries Shug, as the synthetic manufacture of oxygen utilizing quintyllium could have calamitous results.

Oxygen has been manufactured in the laboratory for many years now, processes such as heating mercuric oxide or potassium chlorate to moderately high temperatures. It can also be produced by the electrolysis of water, a process that reverses the violent hydrogen-oxygen reaction often observed in rocket propulsion engines of days-gone-by. An economic method, and therefore popular, is the liquefaction and distillation of air. But, all of this is academic. To produce oxygen on a global scale would take decades using these processes. If the problem remains unsolved, bio-organisms on this world have less than a decade to live. Is it unsolvable?

If you can get your head around the techie bit, without losing your bottle, the rest of this adventure will be a walk in the park.

Chapter 10

The Siren Initiative? Some of the ballads, or laments to use the proper term, were so entrancing that the haggii could use them to lure humans to their deaths. The initiative worked like this – a haggii squad would rise very early, way before breakfast, sometimes it was still dark. The morning mist would settle like a blanket over the mountains reflecting the pre-dawn light as it slowly bathed and massaged the rocks and heather.

The leader would track down a human hunting party, and make sure they saw him. They would give chase. Every Siren

runner could easily escape, but ensured that they ran slowly enough for the hunters to keep up. The runner would lead them to within earshot of the Haggettes to hear the lament – three Haggettes, six vocal chords, meant that fantastic harmonising could be used to achieve melodies that no human could resist. The song that had the most devastating effect was Anthem.

Anthem

Open up your heart
Open up your soul
Do this and it will be a start
Time has taken its toll
That youth from the distant past
Time to meet him again, time to make it last

All the ones you loved so dearly
Look on you from Heaven now
Will see them again – one day
They wait for you, guardians over you
Your light burns so very very bright
Never be out of mind or out of sight

Shifting sands caught in time
Perpetual dusk a place where destiny works
Put yourself first look down from upon high
Use the wings she gave you, time to fly

Open up your heart
Open up your soul
Do this and it will be a start
Time has taken its toll
That youth from the distant past
Time to meet him again, time to make it last

They would wander blindly in the mist towards the source of the melody, and... off the edge of the mountain to their deaths. It worked wonderfully, and the human hunting parties had been greatly reduced over the last few years as a result.

* * *

An emergency meeting of the Senate was called to debate the findings of FEPAC.

The Central Senate of Nations, aka CSN, was formed from the World's governments to resolve issues that no nation, or continent, could reach agreement on. The Senate was made up of the leaders of each nation and included two senior members from each nation's military and judiciary. This was the highest legal establishment on the planet, if it couldn't be resolved in the lower courts and parliaments, it was certainly resolved here, the place where the ubiquitous Buck stops. Ben stormed through the doors, accompanied by Calculus Haggis and Prebble Haggis, exuding anger and remorse. It should never have come to this. The president of the senate this year was Sxsaxjsxjsx of the Oraxonites. The presidency was renewed every three years to ensure balance of judgements and transparency of decisions. Two Oraxonites, whom Ben didn't know or had never seen, sat either side. Spitfire Bob was there with Vibex and

ArundleSprocketSphere. All the other nations were represented also; the Icaria, the Hezmanni, and the Traxons, to name but a few.

Ben addressed the Chair; 'We've just returned from FEPAC, I imagine news of our findings has preceded us?'

Bob answered Ben directly not giving the chair its due or respect. Ben sighed knowing it would be a futile and soul-destroying debate. 'The FEPAC findings leave us with only one choice. A choice that will save billions of lives, you have to understand'

'Have to understand? exclaimed Ben, What about the lives that will be lost? What about the homes that will be destroyed, the lands laid waste? *You* have to understand!'

'Ben, the decisions have been taken, the miners are en route as we speak, you can't oppose us... no one can oppose us.'

Sxsaxjsxjsx continued, 'the Oraxonites have been instructed to act as defenders for the mining project, we have been empowered to ensure no one comes between the miners and the quintyllium.

'The Oraxonites have been instructed? The Oraxonites have been empowered?' Ben thundered.

'The word of this court is Law, decisions taken and instructions handed down will be obeyed. Your carnaptious attitude cannot, and will not, be acknowledged, sit down!'

'Sit down? Right!' Ben composed himself and chose his words carefully; 'it's easy to see that the Oraxonites and the Humans are

102

in cahoots, some kind of pact has been formed, so I choose my words carefully, we will War-Down the Oraxonites, we will War-Down the humans, and we will War-Down any other nation or rabble that attempts to destroy our lands. We have many allies here, all of whom I'm sure, will join us once again in the noble fight to save our people and our land.' And with that, he and Calculus and Prebble Haggis turned and stormed out.

'Remember the Highland Clearances?' asked Prebble Haggis.

'I'm still trying to forget them, my old friend!'

* * *

Tiberius arrived. It must be trendy hour. He assumed his usual position, in front of the fireplace, ready to take up debate.

'Well Benjamin, how does it feel to be one thousand years old?'

'No worse than being nine hundred and ninety-nine, and probably no different to being one thousand and one. You'll know for yourself sooner than you think young haggis.'

The party was going well. As expected. Most of Benjamin's friends were either musicians or magicians and in some cases, both. This was always the recipe for a brilliant time for everyone. Even Benjamin had picked up his beloved mandolin for a brilliant rendition of 'Wha's Like Us'. He hadn't played, in public anyway, for many years but had been secretly practicing for tonight's performance, and Shug knew it. The fluidity and roundness of the very complex middle-eight was a dead give-away. There was probably only one other Haggis on the planet that could achieve this. Brilliant!

'Hamish! Are you listening?' shouted Shug.

Hamish pulled his massive head from the vat of water he had just been dunking for apples in with the fawns. He dropped an apple from his toothless gums and answered with a discordant 'What?'

'You're missing the show – come over here and give us a song and stop messing around with the infants.'

Benjamin thrust his mandolin into Hamish's mitts and shouted 'PLAY!' He strummed a few disjointed chords and plucked a few random notes, 'What do you want to hear, I can't think of anything?'

'Can you play 'Far Far Away'? a sarcastic voice shouted from the balcony. 'Or how about 'Silent Night'?' another equally derisive voice from the fireside.

'Don't you listen to them,' chimed in Tiberius, 'how about a nice Strathspey?' 'Ahhh,' whispered Hamish as he crescendoed into one of his very favourite songs 'The Blue Misty Hills of Glen Shee' with its nice round bouncy tempo – '**heavy**-light-*medium*-light, **heavy**-light-*medium*-light…' Marvellous!

For all his clumsiness and being slower off the mark than most, Hamish had a uncanny natural feel for the mandolin, and most other stringed instruments for that matter; the gentle brush of his strumming, the canny upstrokes of his minor sevenths, the light and shade he brought to every song – inspirational. His singing voice too wasn't that shabby, could hold his own with many more accomplished 'warblers'. As he finished a resounding roar and frenzied applause ran round the room – everyone getting to their feet to show their appreciation. 'How was it?' Hamish shouted over to Shug always seeking his approval. 'Your usual brilliant self – what can I say?, keep that up and you'll be replacing me in the Icarus Paradox!'

'And ninthly…' Tiberius was off on one of his 'pointless' debates with some of the older guests. He knew they were doing it just to wind him up, but played along anyway, 'cause he knew it gave them a bit of fun… if only for a short while.

'So, what do *you* think?'

Shug hadn't been listening, 'what are you arguing about, now?

'What? Have you been on holiday, or something?' 'The humans… will they go ahead with the mining?'

'Yes. They will go ahead, thousands of haggii will die, war will break-out the world will never be the same again.'

'Whoa there! Break it to me gently, why don't you?' replied Tiberius. 'Can't really be what you think Shug, surely?'

Shug gave a wry smile and stared into middle-distance.

'Ah, the futility of youth', sighed Benjamin. 'You need to look at all the angles, young haggii! If they do drive the mines, what will happen? They may get enough oxygen to sustain life, but at what cost? Remember, never confuse price and cost. The price is very low; a few million £'s wages for mining scabs. The cost, however, is very much greater. Famine, disease, death. Wars within wars, battles within battles. Back to the dark ages. I can't subscribe to your interpretation, Shug; they may be stupid, but not that stupid.'

* * *

He stole some time to think about the swing a cat thing. It was a tight space. Who would want to swing a cat anyway? Given the length of a cat including its tail and the average length of a haggis's arm you'd probably need a radius of about 6ft he thought. Would it just be a normal cat or one of the big one's? Is it a standard unit of measure; a cats tail equals 6ft for instance? You know, like a furlong, or engineer's chain, or a piece of string, or a Fluid Ounce. Fluid Ounce was a strange measure. Typically American – who else measure a fluid by weight? Like; is a fluid ounce of water the same weight as a fluid ounce of Mercury? or Air? Bizarre. Swinging around and around must be painful for the cat. Hang on! Cat is also short for catalyzer, like they used in old automobiles with internal combustion engines. Swinging a catalyzer? An even more unlikely pursuit. Hold on a minute! A cat was also the name given to a type of whip used for punishing unruly sailors on the high seas. Cat-O-Nine Tails - so called because there were nine tongues on this whip. Could it leave scars on the sailor's back like cat's scratches? As ships got smaller and faster, attempting to punish a sailor must have gotten more difficult in the increasingly smaller space on the ship. Hence 'not enough room to swing a cat.' Yesss, Shug had it!

Part V – Miners & Mining

Chapter 11

Parrots, parrots, parrots. They were everywhere. The noise was deafening – what is going on? At this time of the morning? And in this rain?

Just about every racer at the last few rounds had copied the hyperslider. Many were beginning to challenge Shug in the early stages, making him pull out all the stops to stay ahead making him lean so far over in the tighter corners round the mountain his shoulder was scraping the rocks resulting in some nasty, painful wounds.

He had awoken early, the idea burning a hole in his brain. The streets were wet from the cold rain that had hammered down thruthenight. Rushing across slippery cobbles the indigo sky threw his darting shadow before him, quiet anticipation building, raging excitement growing. Dawn he decided, was OK too and although preferring the tranquillity of dusk, he couldn't suppress the fascinating respect he felt for the optimism of dawn.

The whole thing was mapped out in his head as he turned the key in the lock of the dilapidated tenement that housed his workshops. Engaging the breakers the vast space was drowned in brilliant white light, exposing a state-of-the-art facility that belied the exterior surroundings and was as out-of-place in this place as an Oraxonite in a comedy club. As sights go it was inspiring in this, the seediest part of the seediest town this side of Hadrian Haggis's Wall.

Did he have enough quintyllium ore? Enough titanium-nimonic alloy? Were the milling cutters tough enough? Was there enough time? A million questions racing through his mind, brain exploding and drums pummelling in his head with no assured outcome or reply. It didn't matter, as always the best that can be done will be done and anything else is a bonus.

Chapter 12

The Universe is now, withnoboutadoubtit, absurdly weird and inescapably forever, doomed. They had done the experiments, the engineers, scientists, and academicians that is. And if, worlds are hurtling away from each other at speeds beyond the comprehension of even an intellectual giant like Newton-Haggis, where does that leave us?

The mathematics have it. The simulations have it. So, at some-when-in-space and some-where-in-time, the cosmos will run out of steam, petre-out, deflate, and come to a lubricated tiptoe-in-the-tulips death... halt.

Ten million years from now? He didn't believe a word of it, the thoughts of doomandgloom not distracting him from the task at hand. The steam hammer dull'ly and explosively thudded, milling cutters screeched, and the welding torch schafuufted as he forged, cast, machined, trepanned, and fabricated the logical extension of components to supersede, nay augment, the hyperslider; 'hyperslider plus' could see the free-view hollovision advert already. The next race was in two weeks, his shoulder badly torn and bruised. He didn't know if he could compete. The hyperslider for his shoulder would certainly protect the gaping wound. It was sleeker and more aerodynamic than the original. Also, he had introduced deflectors that, although wouldn't cause any extra friction to slow him, would give extra grip from sideways forces, the so-called lateral accelerations. These were designed to keep him going if he had any lapses of concentration that would previously have ended in tears. He hated crashing.

Are the laws of physics the same at all places in the universe? At all times in the universe? Was ¾SofL possibly impossible? Was it a pipe dream? Nothing wrong with pipe-dreams. For every one hundred pipe-dreams you have, at least one has to come true. Surely?

The Miners in their thousands descended on the mountain. Humans armed to the teeth with tunnelling and ore extraction equipment to mine the quintyllium they needed to replenish the oxygen supplies of the world. The mine shafts were being driven deep into the mountain to gain access to the richest seams. The road-headers used to do this were massive. Twenty-tonnes or more in weight and about the length of three double-decker buses put end-to-end. Shiny polished steel gleamed in the morning sun.

Large spherical discs covered with hundreds of eight-inch long picks spun at many thousands of revolutions per minute on the ends of huge telescopic arms at the front of the machine. These picks were like shark's teeth and would drill and gnaw and gnash at the rocks to bore the 60 foot diameter tunnels that were required to get the Shearers to the face-line that would be used to mine the 'ore'. The shearers made the road-headers look like Tonka toys. They would extract 20,000 tonnes of rock per minute, which would be processed to gain about 1kg of quintyllium. The same amount of rock that's used to construct an eighteen-storey block of flats - just to get the equivalent of two bags of sugar's worth of quintyllium? Seem a bit bizarre to you? There must be a better way? There was a better way, *there is a better way.*

With all this mining going on, you must be wondering what's happening to the haggis' homes and villages?

Destroyed. Nothing, the humans decided, could stand in the way of their human-rights to get more oxygen. Nothing! 'Human' rights? What about Haggii rights? And, the rights of the entire animal and vegetable Kingdoms?

The first mountain to be 'taken-over' was lucky-white-heather enough to be Ben's mountain. Many of the Haggii Clans in the North had become aware of events and had amassed huge armies and begun the long march South to Ben Nevis. War, at this point, was inevitable. They would reach the mountain, double-timing it, in under two days. There would be nothing left in two days, pondered Shug.

The Sun set. Darkness arose. Fires raged allnight.

At dawn the next day, Shug & Ben stood on the highest peak of Ben Nevis and surveyed the devastation. At twenty-nine thousand and thirty-five feet it was the highest summit on the planet. A thick fog of dust from the mining hung over the mountain like the cloud of eternal sorrow. Fires were merely embers now, glowing crimson through the smog, a thousand haggii homes destroyed. Many souls were lost - Haggii that had stayed-put when the miners moved in. They knew full well the dangers of subsidence, fire, and low explosives, quietly anticipating the storm that was brewing. They had paid a heavy cost but maybe, pondered Ben, a better way to go:- quick, easy, and painless. They would never know the grief and suffering they left behind. The suffering was here but the grief hadn't arrived yet, but for sure, was in the ether.

They looked at each other, and then back at the devastation. Nothing was said for a while. They both knew the war had begun, and just a matter of time before it spread beyond the borders of Nevis and reached the entire nation.

'Tragedy is more tragic as you get older.'

Shug didn't answer. Wasn't sure if it was a question or a declaration but was filled with dread regardless, contemplating what fate the coming days held for him and the haggii nation. Had to deal with it, sort out the immediate problems – **'aggression not depression!'**

You see, nobody knew what would happen when they smashed the quintyllium. To get the oxygen they required meant splitting the element at a sub-atomic level, cleaving the atoms into electrons, protons, and neutrons, (quarks, terrifyingly enough, may not be a figment of the bearded sandal-wearing academician's imaginations), with production of new isotopes with uncertain stability - certain. Would these be harmless or harmful? What effect would this have on the Haggii? What effect would it have on the humans and other specie for that matter?

There were the doom-and-gloom brigade who prophesised the end of everything – Armageddon, the great plague, death of a thousand swords, and Dante's Inferno rolled into one. The scientists were convinced that fall-out would be confined to a ten thousand square mile area in the immediate vicinity of the 'experiment', i.e. the homeland of the Haggii nation. The politicians, in their Macavellian way, said that there would be acceptable losses in equipment, infrastructure, and life.

Shug didn't subscribe to any of these absurd notions. The scientists were sycophants to the politicians, who in turn were sycophants to the military, who, had such a genetic need to remain in power, would say anything to ensure the politicians won the popular vote.

In the nether regions of the lowlands, the slyest of sly debates was happening that would inexplicably alter the course of the crisis entirely, and history, forever. Spitfire Bob, Vibex, and a few cronies were meeting with an Oraxonite diplomatic party to hammer out an agreement on the Haggii Nation or, what would be left of it when the mining ceased.

'The entire Nation?' enquired Eric.

'No, all the lands to the West and the North will be cleared for your people,' answered Bob, 'the rest will be scavenged – reclaimed – for the Haggii. The CSN will police the borders, keep the peace, and ensure you have the Lion's share of the rebuilding and infrastructure projects. It will be yours to keep, colonise forever.'

'You can't be serious!' You expect me to go head-to-head with the Haggii, and in return, I get a measly few million acres? Or, should I say, an obliterated few million acres requiring extensive rebuilding?'

Vibex butted in; 'I agree, for the pact to be workable, the Oraxonites should be gifted the entire country – lock-stock-and-barrel. You know dividing the land will lead to conflicts that will never be resolved – never be lost or won.' Vibex was right, refreshingly enough – sadly, one of his clearer moments. It was a given that the Haggii would fight tooth and nail to the last beast standing; no one would give-up-the-ghost.

'Gifted?' responded Eric, I wouldn't call the prospect of a million of my countrymen slain, a gift. Do you?'

'OK, OK,' enough said Bob, you will have the entire country for your assistance, and what happens to the Haggii, will be my problem.'

'Maybe we could ship them off to Oraxonos?'

No one laughed. It wasn't funny, but the irony was palpable.

As the plan unfolded it was clear to see that many beasts would be killed. Two battalions of Oraxonites were to be disembarked immediately for the lower haggii mountains, where the mining was beginning, to protect the miners. In parallel, Eric would return to Oraxonos for the invasion and colonisation of Alba.

When the Oraxonites had left the castle, Bob addressed Vibex;

'Firstly – don't ever question my decisions in front of an enemy, EVER! And secondly, I don't give you enough information to have a valid opinion on these matters, so don't have one. And lastly, listen up now, I'm about to tell you the real plan do you think you could play ball?'

'Yes sir,' replied Vibex, 'absolutely.'

'You'd better had, or you'll be joining a million dead haggii!'

* * *

Another techie bit, (you can skip this if you like; it's your funeral).

Most organisms depend on oxygen to sustain their biological processes. The great majority of living organisms fall into two categories - in the first are the higher plants like the Thistle, and the photosynthetic bacteria, organisms that utilize light energy to combine carbon-dioxide and water into more complex materials, but mainly carbohydrates, and at the same time they release oxygen into the atmosphere; this is called photosynthesis. The second category is the higher animals, most microorganisms, and photosynthetic cells that live in the dark. All these second-category organisms use a process called enzyme-catalyzed oxidation using materials such as glucose as the fuel and oxygen as the terminal-oxidizing agent, (metabolism). The end products of metabolism in these organisms are carbon dioxide and water, which are returned to the atmosphere.

Listen, the net result of these functions is the *oxygen cycle*. The photosynthetic organisms ingest carbohydrates and give off oxygen and the aerobic organisms ingest oxygen and give off carbon dioxide. Perfect! Around three and a half trillion tons of carbon dioxide is cycled annually via these processes; that's 3,500,000,000,000 tons!

All specie in the animal kingdom need oxygen to sustain metabolism and thus life. Air is inhaled and oxygen in the air is exchanged in the lungs between the atmosphere and the hemoglobin in the blood. The blood carries the oxygen to all parts of the body in which metabolic processes occur. It also carries carbon dioxide back to the lungs, where the carbon dioxide is exchanged with the atmosphere and exhaled. Easy, eh?

If the oxygen concentration were to drop to about half its value in the atmosphere no species would survive, and as it looks, the outlook's bleak. Shug suspects the humans have a lot to answer for.

Enter Quintyllium. The more metal-rich oxides are metallic conductors and tend to be nonstoichiometric; that is, they are observed to exist over a range of compositions all possessing the same underlying structure. A number of the quintyllium oxides exhibit more than one crystal structure (polymorphism). Quintyllium is studied extensively by the elders because of its 'interesting magnetic, electrical, and organic properties'.

Ben needed to meet with all the Nation's leaders, especially Spitfire Bob. If he could get the main protagonists around the table, he knew a resolution could be reached. He had to ensure the human military and politicians were not involved. He needed – Bob, for sure, Magdalena - High Priestess of the Dolphins, Herod King of the Hezmanni, and Sxsaxjsxjsx of the Oraxonites. It would take time:- Time his nation didn't have. If he could stop the mining for a couple of weeks, it would buy him enough time to gather the heads-of-state from around the globe so an agreement could be hammered out. Bob could raise an injunction on the mining to buy him this time.

Ben had travelled to the Lowlands to try and talk some sense into Spitfire Bob. It was late when he arrived and he was duly ushered through chamber after chamber, hall after hall until he reached the rooms that were the nerve centre of the Human Monarchies' Palace.

His office was awesome. Floor-to-ceiling green tinted bullet proof glass overlooking the dirty old city he had systematically destroyed and then nurtured with agonising patience to the masterpiece it is today. Glass, Neon, Concrete, Steel. The sky was clear and the eye could see to the edge of the curvature. City of tiny lights. Flashing airship landing lights blinked in the distance. One hundred and nine storeys below taxis honked and beeped and people scurried hither-and-thither oblivious of the storm brewing that would become a fundamental part of their lives. The night would harbinger intelligent beasts and intelligent people making unintelligent decisions.

'Come in Ben, it's late, nightmares from too much cheese for your supper keeping you awake?' Bob wasn't a wordsmith.

'No, I don't eat cheese, stick to ginger-wine and vindaloo escargot at this time of night,' said Ben, trying to ensure Bob thought he was receptive to the banter, knowing that it was polite to get the small talk out of the way before delivering requests.

Bob laughed, his usual cackley, infectious chuckle before pursing his lips, narrowing his eyes, and engaging an all-together seriously serious look. 'What can I do for you, my old friend?' Ben had lost his stutter when he was very young, maybe just turned one hundred years, but could feel it galloping towards him at a ferocious pace. 'Calm down', he thought to himself, 'don't let him intimidate you; everyone is depending on you... me!' At the very moment Ben had Bob's ear the doors to the inner-sanctum were thrown open, no announcement necessary, Vibex had arrived. He stormed past in a flurry of cape, sword, body armour, and self-importance.

Suddenly, and with more than mild surprise, the adrenalin kicked-in hitting him head-on like the express train to AuchenShuggle. He stood-up, strode forward, shoulder charging Vibex aside, smashed a priceless relic with his staff, and roared - 'the fallout will kill my kinsmen!'

No stutter. Unbelievable.

* * *

Shug was at the Loch of Miracoli when he heard of the meeting between Ben and Bob and Vibex. Seething with rage was a mild way to describe his mood. The sun rise over the Loch was just beginning to turn the sky a brilliant orange as another uncertain day dawned. Usually he would only come here at dusk, but the news had left him thinking of the difference in beasts and people approach to… well… life. He felt another equation in the offing so had to get some solitude. He thought of the extremes of traits held by all; on the one hand the beings who would work hard who would strive to be the best they could be, who consciously made sure they gave something back to their society and their country. And on the other, the exact opposite of this – the scroungers and the free loaders and the lazy and the stupid. Was there a link to intelligence here, like his infamous premise between intelligence and cunning?

He paddled some more as the sun cleared the trees on the far banks. It would be hot today, must only be about nine o'clock and the temperature soaring,' he whispered to himself thinking 'time to set-off for work.' The banks glistened as the sun skipped off the red sands and ricocheted into the air giving a strange hazy shimmer in front of the mountainous backdrop.

Some more paddling and intense soul searching later he had a framework to link these, or at least, a nebulous framework. What if we consider the two extremes, (he liked extremes), and call these – to the right 'work-proud,' and to the left 'work-shy.' Then, superimpose on this at the lowest level 'decreasing intelligence' and at the highest 'increasing intelligence.' He scrambled to the banks and started scribbling furiously in the damp sand.

'Right,' excitement was building, 'if I think of how beings are and how they think and behave and placed them in one of the quadrants what do I have?'

He concentrated deeply, scooped up and swallowed a large handful of water to quench his thirst and soothe a throbbing head and continued. Although he could place certain acquaintances in the top right quadrant and in the bottom left quadrant, the top left and the bottom right quadrants remained empty. 'This is wrong - rather than placing everyone in a scatter type format, is this problem in fact a continuum? Does everyone lie on a line through the quadrants? Shug thought of a diagonal line running from bottom left corner to top right – too simple, what about a parabola? Again, it doesn't capture the extremes of intelligence and attitude to life. *Is it* asymptotic? This was abstract in the extreme, but worth spending a little time on. The more intelligence someone has the more likely they'll have an aptitude to improving themselves and giving something back? If this hypothesis is true, then the opposite must be said for the less intelligent species. No this isn't right – Shug knew many and had many friends that weren't quite shining stars in the scheme of things but would move heaven and earth to help you if you were down on your luck. They were also very resourceful when the push came to the shove. So maybe not – but, in general the asymptotic curve would run true for maybe eighty–ninety percent of the population. Asymptotic, he reminded himself, means getting ever closer to an extreme but never ever reaching it. Imagine standing forty feet from a wall and with every step you took you were only allowed to cover half the distance you covered on your previous step – you would never reach the wall – this is 'asymptotic.' The friends he just thought of would lie in the bottom right quadrant – and it would follow that there would be some other 'outliers' that would fall into the top left quadrant but the majority would fall on the curve.

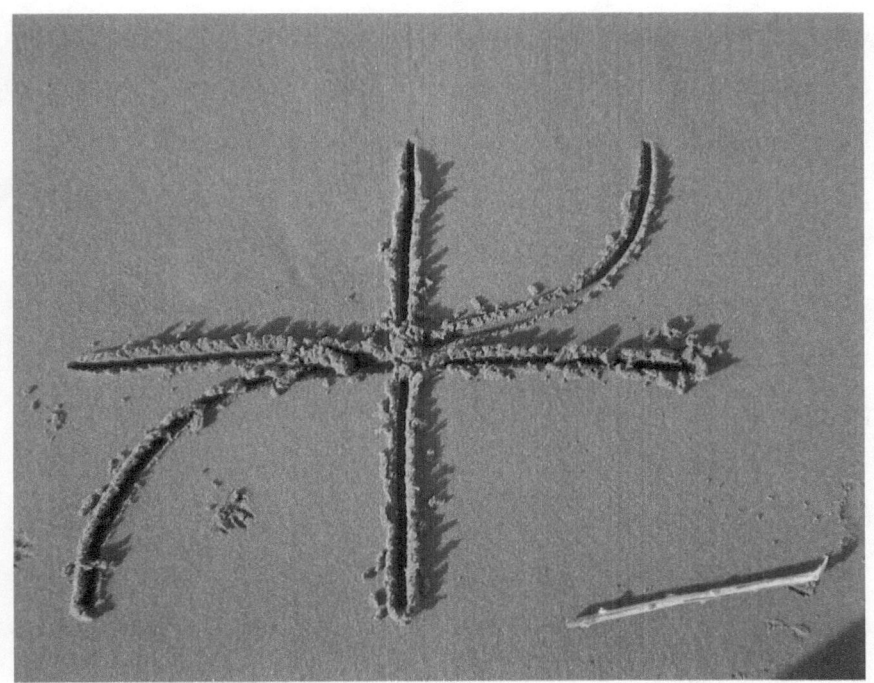

This, he thought, would be called "The Asymptotic Curvilinear." Elegance personified!

The day passed quickly, everyone at work talking about the invasion and the mining and the Elders. Shug struggled.

Sick as a Parrot? Do parrots get sicker than other creatures, he thought? They have sad eyes; keep looking at you and then looking down, kind of bashful which could be construed as poorly? Maybe. Or did it mean the infamous Captain Two-Pistols Parrot. He was renowned for getting so drunk during Christmas festivities, he'd be violently ill all the way to summer! No, too corny! Shug once saw an elephant being sick from over excerption in one of the races and it was a huge amount. Didn't stop for ages, all green and yellow and sticky. Couldn't imagine a parrot being sick like that. Maybe the parrot's sick was projectile and therefore deserved the cliché to be named after it. How far could a parrot project its vomit? Was there a world record? No, barking up the wrong tree here. There was the infamous green parrot disease that could be passed to haggii making them very sick. 'As sick as a haggis?' Doesn't quite have the same ring. Shug started thinking of 'sick' in a metaphorical sense. Could it mean 'melancholy'? That is, not to be physically sick but to be down-hearted, depressed? *Possibly*, could be on the right track here. Shug paddled around for a while perusing over the possible explanations he had arrived at. All a bit too straight and narrow, needed to think a bit more laterally. 'I'm sure I've read somewhere that when parrots get sick and are making a recovery, they will eat anything, including rotten fruit' he said to himself. We all know that fruit ferments, and that rotten fruit is in the advanced stages of fermentation, i.e. producing alcohol. So if a parrot ate this, and was poorly anyway, wouldn't the alcohol make it drunk very quickly, maybe to the point of passing-out? Like Two Pistols? Then… the next day the parrot would be ill from the virus it had or whatever and ill from the effects of the alcohol too… hung-over if you like, hence; 'as sick as a parrot'!

Yesss, Shug had it!

Part VI – In the Beginning

Chapter 12b

The evening was about to explode into, what was to be remembered as the reason for the war that ended everything. Everything! Space, time, fire, water... *being*.

That was now, this is then.

Projectile weapons had been outlawed centuries earlier. There had been decades of bloodied and futile wars, millions died in the name of organised religion. Then, someone had a question that put many extremists on the back foot – 'why do we have to kill and keep on killing?'

The Heads of the world's nations came together to draw up a treaty that would put an end to the fighting. Many years were spent 'debating' how and who would police this, who would pay for it, who would benefit from it and who would lose out because of it. One of the main points of contention was the banning of all weapons. After much bickering and late night debate, the directive was diluted and watered down to; 'all projectile weapons.'

In the years up to the treaty weapons had improved immensely. Maybe 'improved' is the wrong word and used out of context in this instance. A better way of describing it is; "they had become extremely effective in accomplishing what they were designed to do." Rifles and pistols - firing steel, titanium, and silver bullets had reached the end of any useful development, that is, they had gotten as good as they were going to get. This paved the way for grenade launchers, mortars, rocket launchers, laser guided rocket launchers, self-guided rocket launchers, and the HDSC rifles that could fire around corners, (HemiDemiSemiCyclotronic). These so-called 'pulse' weapons were used to devastating effect.

So, what was exempt from the ban? Well…, any form of stabbing weapon was OK - swords, daggers, and spears. Also the humble bow and arrow and catapults were OK too. Granted, these are projectile weapons, but nothing like the scale of destruction could be had with these as that that could be had with the other weapons described.

The treaty worked. Peace settled over the planet for three millennia. Civilisations developed, poverty and famine were all but eradicated. The nye-on-exhausted ecosystems began to heal.

It was a good time to live and grow and learn.

Everyone worked hard and played hard, leisure time was an extremely precious commodity. Government money was spent on the worthwhile things in life and not on the military. Many billions of each Nation's hard earned currency was invested in medical research, advanced clean fuel technologies for travel, industrial and domestic use, animal welfare, and, the still elusive theories of time travel and DeessemReessem, (physically disassembling an organism at an atomic level and reassembling it somewhere else; across the room, in a different country, or on a different continent). DeessemReessem was theoretically feasible and scientifically proven, but the energies and costs involved precluded any commercial application of the technology. This will change.

Disease and illness was a thing of the past. There were very few germs or viruses they didn't have solutions for, the fuels were clean and efficient, air quality improved across the globe, and the animals were treated with the respect they deserved. As a matter-of-fact many animals were responsible for the research and development of these new technologies. Time travel had been promised for decades now, but the scientists were still miles away from anything that could be described as a workable solution.

The years became decades and in turn centuries. Millennia passed and all was well. Life was sweet.

It wasn't until the humans came to the Haggii Nation's shores that things began to change. The haggii were a peaceful race and were willing to share the land with the humans, but they got greedy, grasping more and more until eventually the haggii were outcast to the barn wastelands of the North. Many were killed, there was mass suffering. 'Miserable wretches capitalising on a race's misery,' Prebble Haggis had once noted.

Looking back, it was easy to reminisce and be embroiled in hopeless romanticism. The future is rarely regarded as bright; the past by contrast, is seen as glowing, growing more lustrous the further back you look. Of course, some moments from the past deserve a long retrospective gaze; Prebble Haggis is good at this, but rubbish at romanticism.

* * *

The Battle for Oraxonos turned out to be the coldest bloodiest battle in the Nation's history. The Oraxonites outnumbered the Haggii ten-to-one. The humans thought that the easier option was to leave the Haggii and Oraxonites to slog it out; they could annihilate each other whilst they got on with the mining, what if a few million haggii died?

The haggii clans amassed on the North side of the plain that would eventually become known as, ingeniously enough:- Battlefield. On the South and the East gathered the Oraxonite warriors.

The morning air was cool and fresh; the combined effect of the gentle rains and honey scented dew. The skies were dark; orange and blue thunderclouds amassing in the West, shafts of sunlight cleaving through them like humungous swords scything through fields of swaying wheat.

It was intense.

Eric of the Oraxonites, and Benjamin of the Haggii Nation came together in the middle of the battleground. Could there be a truce? The Oraxonites didn't need oxygen but did need more land. Oraxonos was massively overpopulated, overmined, and underfunded. They too coveted Alba with envious eyes. Why not let the Humans annihilate the Haggii? This would leave their country more susceptible to a successful invasion? King Bob and the human government (FDR - Federation for Democratic Reform), had decreed that if the Oraxonites did not sabotage their quintyllium route for the replenishment of oxygen, they would be given the Alba and the wastelands of Arctic to expand their race, the much needed 'room to breed.' Would this be enough? We know how riddled with greed they are – time will tell. Time always tells.

Alba as we know is beautiful, but you wouldn't wish Arctic on your worst enemy. Life is so stark and minimalist that any being *exists*; they do not live. The thin end of the harshest wedge? But, this was a better bet than what any imagined Oraxonite future could be; famine, starvation, disease, and eventually; extinction. But given Eric's rendezvous with Spitfire

Bob and the promises of him having Alba too – there wasn't the slightest chance of a truce.

There was no common ground. Eric and Benjamin returned to there respective armies, the battle would be fought to a conclusion as planned.

Chunderous drums from both armies echoed like thunder around the battlefield. Each army sang their respective Anthems and each Warrior recited prayers to their respective God. The swirl of the Pipes was haunting. Shug looked into the orange skies – the clouds more beautiful and dramatic than he'd ever seen, the light at the edges of the clouds from the distant sun adding to the effect. What was that called? The light around the edge of a cloud?, creptula rays? crespular rays? crepucular rays? Oh, damn it! He couldn't think – but it didn't matter, this could be the last cloudscape he would ever behold.

The Oraxonite archers struck the first blow, the skies darkening with a hundred thousand arrows airborne. The Haggii dropped to their knees and raised their shields above their heads. Most arrows were stopped, only a few getting through, but with disastrous results. The poisoned titanium tips on these ensured that even a flesh wound would be fatal. Haggii archers responded in a fifteen-minute exchange of about a hundred million arrows, each army doing about the same amount of damage.

The haggii ranks divided; one half heading towards the archers in the East, the other towards the infantry in the North. The Oraxonites charged to meet them, their archers still launching arrows high into the air. These would kill both Oraxonites and Haggii, but expounded Eric, 'the losses *would* be acceptable'. The front ranks of both armies collided with such force and ferocity that bones were broken and skulls crushed by the impact. The dull thud of swords on shields, the tolling of axes on armour reverberated around the battlefield. Shug had killed maybe ten or eleven Oraxonites, when suddenly the biggest ugliest Oraxonite he had ever seen charged towards him. In a series of movements that segued together he side stepped the flailing sword, grabbed the monster by the mane pulling him forwards and downwards, bringing his sword down on the back of his neck with a force that hacked through glistening tissue compacted muscle and brittle bone, cleanly, leaving the still-living head in his clenched fist. Adrenalised anger and venomous fury pulsated through every muscle in his body. Stepping back, another attacker was upon him. He beat this new attacker to a messy pulp using the severed head to great effect, spinal chord and cerebrum fluids gushing everywhere. He exalted the loudest roar of the day - the loudest roar of the most miserable desolate day of his life.

The battle did not last long. Less than an hour maybe. Both sides suffering horrendous casualties. Many young lives were brought to an abrupt halt.

It was terrible.

The Haggii, however, *were* 'victorious'. They used a technique from days of old, from the battles between their own clans. As the warriors came face-to-face, each Haggis would, whilst protecting himself from the opponent directly in front, kill the Oraxonite adjacent and to his right. This was phenomenally effective and meant that each haggis was killing nine or ten Oraxonites.

About a thousand Oraxonites remained, dug-in in a small fortress at the far north corner of the plain. The Haggii regrouped and Ben approached the last Oraxonite stronghold with two of his generals under a white flag of truce. The fortress gates opened and Eric and two of his officers appeared and marched towards Ben.

'Before you make a decision to sign the death warrant of your remaining warriors, please listen to my terms for your surrender,' said Ben.

After a brief pause, Eric replied with a simple 'go on.'

'If you agree to break the allegiance with the humans stop fighting us you can take your army and return to your homes and villages, you are free to leave.'

'And our weapons.'

'Take them with you, take your flags with you let them fly high, carry them with honour.'

It was an act of compassion not seen in millennia, an act that some day Benjamin Augustus Haggis would come to regret.

But as Eric and his warriors marched from their castle and headed homewards, Shug couldn't help but wonder – 'am I going to be fighting the same Oraxonites on the same battlefield in the not too distant future?'

The battle closed. The skies opened.

Chapter 14

Everyone was preparing for the party. Hogmanay! This was the most important day in the Haggii calendar, which is littered with many glittering social events but none as emotional and soul stirring as this. Hogmanay, the end of the old year – with the opportunity to put any mistakes or disappointments behind you, and the dawn of a new year - with all the joyous hope and bright prospects that that had to proffer.

The hagettes rushed around busily gathering ingredients and foodstuffs for the feast that would ensure everyone has their fill to bursting point. There were the sweetest sugars, fluffiest flours, spiciest spices, sourest salts, lusciousest fruits, and of course, the secret ingredients that had been handed down from fore parents over the millennia that gives haggii food its delicious and exotic essence, (do you think the fiendish alchemy of steaming a thistle or two comes without extensive education and sweat inducing muscle aching heart pummelling hard work)?

The alpha males of the group hunted and gathered the raw ingredients for the feast. The only time a haggii kills another animal in peacetime is for the purpose of eating – it is written, (so shall it be)! The hunting party had a good and fruitful weeks' foraging returning with many bizarre and eclectic specie of animals, fishes, and amphibia.

The pyrotechnologists had been beavering away for months to deliver the best ever firework show that would last the duration of the party. It was a given that, each show, had to be bigger and better than the previous year's show. Tonnes and tonnes of gunpowder, nitrates, sulphates, nitro-glycerines, gelignites, and semtex were being put into the show, not to mention the miles and miles of fuse ribbon. It would be seen for miles, and be so bright that the nightlight would seem like daylight.

And, what about the brewers?

Haggii are exceptional fermenters and first-rate Coopers, and when it comes to concocting a potent potion there is no one nor no species finer. The base spirits for these drinks are distilled, distilled, and distilled again, then left to mature gracefully over many years in massive underground Vats to give the purity and strength required, a prerequisite incidentally, for any Haggii brew, (most partakers get their sight back within three days, bytheway).

What outfit to wear?

This wasn't a question just asked by the female Haggii. No, it was massively important to look your best on Hogmanay, everyone was on show and anyone that was anyone in the haggii world would be there, that is, many paparazzi baiters would be in attendance. For the males the best and most colourful tartans, and the poshest sporrans adorned with feathers and furs from birds and carnivores living in faraway places. And the females would be in their best shawls, glitteriest jewellery & accessories, and daintiest shoes.

Beasts of all boroughs – start your engines!

* * *

'They do it because violence is a mental illness. If, in their minds they can't grasp animal empathy they're wounded, bereft if you like. They can't be part of the... they don't feel included.'
The emergency meeting of the Council had been called to debate options available before all-out war was inevitable.

'That's your theory? That's it?' This pissed Ben off. It was an radical viewpoint that was both infantile and highly antagonistic coupled with the fact it was being expounded by young Tiberius, one of his prodigies.

'Have you looked across the mountain this morning? Does the devastation not convince you? Are we not "wounded"? This is the worst yet. They have gone too far this time. The peace we had, the trust, *the harmony* even, are consigned to ashes. One thousand years of building bridges and they can be as crass as this? It beggars belief.'

'I'm not defending or condoning their actions, just trying to put things in perspective. There are only a few extremists, the vast majority is happy to live with us, to keep the peace,' Tiberius continued attempting to defend his viewpoint. 'We can easily beat the extremists – it wouldn't even amount to a skirmish.'

He was no match for Ben, and knew it.

'Skirmish? You weren't on Oraxonos, you didn't see or smell the suffering, you couldn't feel the hopelessness of war... you weren't there.'

Ben sat down, knowing this was going nowhere. Didn't enjoy washing anyone's dirty linen in public. A doubt had been sown, and he would investigate Tiberius' reasoning further – but at the appropriate time, obviously.

'Hagii,' piped up Calculus, 'we need to debate all options open to us on this matter. Now, Tiberius has made his views clear, also, Ben has been just as eloquent in his opposition to these views. I'm sick of learning things the hard way – the facts of life are on the table. Has anyone an alternative to war?' The Forum became eerily silent – 'war', it was now the time when there could be no turning back. 'War?' Many hadn't realised the severity of the debate – not fully, anyhow.

Ben said 'there is an alternative, well, there may be an alternative.' A ripple ran round the Forum, more of a torrent really, words like 'Maybe? Might be? Could be?' reverberated.

Calculus again tried to keep the debate orderly. 'Do you have anything solid, Ben?'

'Shug?' Ben had, in his inimitably subtle manner, given Shug the floor.

'There may be a better way of producing oxygen,' began Shug, 'what isn't exactly an element, and not exactly an organism?' No one answered. Shug continued, 'there may be a way of creating the magnetic field and controlled atmosphere required to have quintyllium give up a certain number of quarks, gain some atomic mass, and set off the reaction to...' He paused, by the vacant looks of the councilors around the hall he knew he wasn't getting through. Although, one brave soul, asked 'reaction to – what?' Ben stepped in to help simplify the proposal for those of less academic persuasion in attendance.

'Shug has a plan, and we would be foolish to rush headlong into anything, without, at least, giving him time to prove us wrong, or him right'.

* * *

'When is a fluid not a fluid?'

Couldn't get it out his head - in the Battle for Oraxonos, the blow that felled the biggest fattest Oraxonite he'd ever seen. Was always of the opinion that you should never, *EVER*, kill another creature unless the principal purpose is food, and even then, only if you're on the dire brink of starvation. Feels guilty already, but knows inside that the beautiful end will justify the brutal means. A single blow to take out such a massive animal? Mesmerising!

He and the other Haggii warriors had to endure the battle over and over again, as filmed by hundreds of the Council's satellite cameras. It was customary to record every battle from the skies to ensure the critics and desk-jockeys could foundlessly berate the protagonists to the n'^{th} degree and keep themselves in a job, *evidently*. The Elders would have us believe that this archaic custom has something to do with learning and improving for the next battle; how was it they put it?, 'We can only use what we have learned if we evaluate what's happened, distil the results, and apply the progression to similar situations truthfully. As Engineers, you of all haggii should know we reduce the issues to first principles and resolve.'

Engineers or Warriors? They were fine lines that, year on year, were blurring to unison.

God, he hoped there would never be another battle.

Smiled ruefully as he remembered BAH's comment of the motion of that single blow being 'virtually balletic, almost fluid'. Poor terms in a time of war, granted, but profundity *was* Benjamin's middle name.

* * *

Fluid? Fluidity? What is a fluid anyway? Another perplexing question?

How can you describe a fluid? Water? Well, of course water is a fluid! What about oil? Again, yes. But is there a difference between heavy gearbox oil and, say, shaving oil?, not that any self-respecting haggii would confess to shaving, (although, secretly, they all always wanted to look their best, so partook in this human practice regardless). Yes is the answer, viscosity mainly. So, something with a viscosity level of zero, like water, is a fluid, whilst something with a viscosity level of one hundred like treacle, isn't?

No, not exactly.

Treacle flows, doesn't it? So it must be a fluid, then!

So, anything that flows is a fluid?

Yes!

Even at an atomic level? So, as the atoms that make up steel are constantly in motion, they too, could be described as a fluid – they flow too?

No. No. No! Too academic, not differentiating enough, not even close – steel is a continuum, dimwit – K.I.S.S!

Shug was getting angry with himself, and to make matters worse, the darker spectra of the composed dusk he was bathing in weren't just the right shade of indigo. Not that that would deflect him from the perplexing question in hand.

If anything that flows is a fluid – we shouldn't just consider liquids then, but gases too?

Seems reasonable… so where does that leave us?

All I need is a definition that describes fluidity, something for everyone to use in everyday use, but nothing that a Quantum Mechanic would spend hours analysing!

OK. Think about water, or, oxygen even – a very current affair! What is happening to the molecules of oxygen as you drag your hand through the air?

They're passing over each other sliding apart with little or no effort.

What's a good analogy?

Maybe a pack of cards, each card sliding over the adjacent card, frictionless – no shear resistance. No shear resistance?, getting warm.

This isn't really much of a description for the common haggii 'though. We need a simple statement – an amorphism ifyoulike for every day use.

Think…..

'A fluid is a substance that cannot resist shear'.

Yesss! Shug had it.

Part VII – Something Has To Give

Chapter 15

Four initiatives were underway and warriors near and far were being summoned and mobilised to march into uncharted territory, to push the envelope of modern warfare and endeavour:- from the North the Haggii armies had formed and had already marched as far as Ben Nevis. Everyone, to a haggis, had no illusions as to the seriousness of the problem. From the North-East the Hezmanni were ready and would march on Haggii City Central if the situation deteriorated further; for millennia they had stood shoulder to shoulder with the Haggii and this millennium would be no different. And, surprisingly enough, from what was left of the Oraxonite armies a reformation was underway, the raggled-taggled remnants ready to support the Haggii initiative, they hated the humans more than they hated the Haggii and Hezmanni combined, so wanted to be part of the plan. But, they can't be trusted which may yet be their downfall. Lastly, the regular Haggii armies were regrouping ready for the murderous onslaught.

* * *

Benjamin was a unique haggis. Shug had no idea how old he was, but guessed at probably around two thousand years which even in haggii terms, is old. Little things that had slipped out in the quiet conversations they had had over the years yielded some significant clues. He spoke respectfully of the Battle of BannockNess, which was way way in the distant past, easily before the Oraxonites left the world, or the humans had invaded our shores. Also, he had lost one of his legs and never confessed any of the details of the incident even when pushed, but Shug suspected it was in battle. Maybe not BannockNess, or *the* War, or

the Battle for Traxon, but in one of the more recent wars for sure.

He wore glasses. Not shades to look cool, but glasses of the seeing kind. To read to travel to watch plays; *you know* every day things. One of Shug's first inventions was Visiotide®, a drug that made the need for glasses obsolete. Ben refused to use it. Even though that with applications to both eyes twice daily for six weeks ninety-nine per cent of haggii regained 20/20 vision, which incidentally, is straight from the Holo' TV advertisement for the product.

'I like my glasses their cool, kinda.'

'Cool my big hairy arse,' thought Shug. Not only were they very very old, they had also been broken-in-half years before and been repaired by taping the two halves together with an old plastobandelast®.

Nevertheless, Ben was unique. The cleverest haggis alive today, and arguably, the cleverest haggis of all time. Had taken Shug under his wing many years previously and had cultivated and nurtured him into the great inventor he was today. Ben is educated in many trades and sciences – biology, biomechanics, chemistry, physics, quantum mechanics, plumbing… you get the idea. Shug had specialised against Ben's advice early on concentrating on physics and biomechanics. Although, to be fair, he had achieved a greater skill with many of the trades in probably around a one hundred year period than most Master Craftsmen would in a lifetime. He liked to consider himself a 'specialist', and enjoyed the satisfaction to-be-had by being very focused.

'You'll have to lead them' said Shug.

'What do you mean, lead?' replied Ben.

'They won't make a decision. Too many cooks and all that. If you don't take centre stage and guide them to the logical conclusion, we're lost.' Shug paused for effect and thought of the manner in which the government was managed. Bureaucracy, politics, red tape, covering-your-back, backstabbing, politics, and more politics. No wonder nothing was ever achieved. Good ideas would be put forward to the various committees, sub-committees, quangos, and work-groups to debate and, after many hours and everyone having their tuppence worth, would re-emerge as shadows of their former selves. Someone had to cut-to-the-chase and lead these faceless, chinless, gormless wasters to a logical conclusion. They would be forced into action and out of inaction.

A meeting of the Federation was scheduled the next morning and as Ben lay awake most of the night thinking of all the possible outcomes and eventualities, he couldn't get Shug's parting words out of his mind, 'You'll have to lead them...'

Ben hadn't had the influence he wished for on FEPAC, but as haggii live years and years longer than humans he had seen many come and go without being able to convince their 'governments' something had to change. This latest discovery had prompted the Chair of the Forum to address Ben. 'Sir, you have more experience and insight than any of us sitting here. You know the implications of not addressing this issue. I plead with you to be our representative, indeed, take my place as Chairman, take the results of our analyses to the CSN and plead for action'. Ben was taken aback. A minute ago he had been drawing smiley faces in his note pad and here he was being asked to lead FEPAC. 'Shiver me timbers!' Not that he was a sailor, or even nautical – but this took him by surprise and he was sure he hadn't the confidence or influence that most of the human scientists enjoyed with the politicians. (No haggis had ever been elected, or had the inclination to be elected, a politician in their governments).

'Sir, I am honoured and humbled by your request, but surely, one of your military advisers is better placed to influence *your* government out of inaction?'

'I disagree Ben, and we need to reach beyond cynicism, it is not 'our' government, but everyone's government. You can explain the complexities of this analysis in a language that the politicians can understand, and hopefully, act upon.'

He thought for a long moment before finally conceding with a heavy sigh; 'if I do this it has to be with the support of the entire Forum, everyone solid… '

'I have already discussed this with all members, sorry, but if you wish a show of hands I'm sure no one would object.'

'No, that won't be necessary..., no, I would request however, a private council with King Bob with no military presence, including ArundleSprocketShere and *especially* Vibex. At this point I will meet with the politicians.'

Ben thought back to the experiment that showed how quickly the oxygen was running out, and the reasons expounded in the subsequent report. Photosynthesis, over population, etc, had been overtaken in the intervening years with the metaphorical finger pointing straight to the selling of vast volumes of oxygen to other worlds. The humans were, as always had been suspected, guilty as sin.

He would approach the CSN.

* * *

Why do lemmings leap off mountains? It was a good question and well worth contemplating in the shallows of Loch Lomness with the pleasant cloak of twilight rising. But was it perplexing enough? Shug was still toying with the question 'Why do cats have nine lives?' seems a little unfair, or how about 'hair of the dog' as an expression – what does that mean? These were eminently more perplexing questions but nowhere near as serious as the poor Lemming problem. The thought had flashed through his mind when he seen a Leap of Lemmings double-timing it North earlier that morning on his way to the Forum. Even the collective noun was somehow derogatory and derisory towards these poor fellows, but Shug couldn't help thinking wryly of the master of wit and ready repartee that had come up with the term, (probably called Roger). So *why do* lemmings jump off cliffs? He only knew a handful of them, so didn't really have a basis for drawing down any definitive conclusions, and hadn't for that matter, ever posed the question to any of the ones he knew.

Is it an ego thing? *JERONIHMO!,* and then throwing yourself head first into the great void between grassy cliff-top and raging froth buffeted ocean, and all your pals not wishing to be outdone, gracefully following suit? Don't be soft! The one's he knew were all more sensible and conservative than this.

Lionel, one of the older lemmings Shug got friendly with had once let it slip that this was the only way a Lemming could die with honour. At the time, he remembered thinking – 'that's strange, a bit of a change of subject to the subject we are debating; the pros-and-cons of missing out the middle game in a game of Chess, that is, going straight from the opening game to the end game,' – (a bit radical but preferred by many of the great Haggii chess masters, incidentally). And when probed as to the sudden change in topic, Lionel didn't answer but made a funny gesture

159

with his left eyebrow and curled the edge of his top lip before staring into middle distance. Was this an analogy for chess? They lived their lives in a very measured and mathematical fashion; assessing each situation, giving it its due attention, deriving many possible solutions, running them past their peer group, placing each solution in order of riskiness, and then, and only then, implementing a risk free decision. They followed this path whether deciding on stomping to war or nipping down the grocers for a pint of milk. Strange but true.

Well *OK* well, ego or bravado could be ruled out as an answer to the question. Was it a way of impressing the female of the species? A bit drastic not to put too fine a point on it, and surely the young would-be brides would have formed a movement to stop potential mates jumping off faraway cliffs? Some weird and wonderful sisterhood of lemmings burning their underwear! He was stretching the sublime to the ridiculous. There must be a reason!

Honour? What was it Lionel had said about honour? There were many creatures across the animal kingdoms that worshipped strange and wonderful Gods or Demigods and had historical references written in their Chronicles that there was a beautiful life to be had after death. Apparently, this would be had in a wonderful land where fruits are numerous & succulent, companions are athletic and gorgeous, and they will partner any follower that dies a martyr's death in this wonderful land. Surely not?, not the Lemmings?

Shug was entering a bizarre place where bizarre thoughts should be harnessed and kept in a small box in a quiet corner of the thinkers mind, until a time when they could be debated rationally when a better foundation of the questions posed could be better understood and subsequently dealt with. Now wasn't that time.

The purple twilight had morphed into an indigo night, the dark depths of the Loch becoming murky and rapidly cooling, chilling Shug to the bone and reminding him that for tea he had a gallon of piping hot pterodactyl broth simmering. For the first time, astonishingly enough, he hadn't solved one of his own perplexing questions – but by being presented with the complexity of this seemingly innocent conundrum, he was pleased to store it away for an appropriate time, when he had the experience, education, and learning to answer it with the gravitas it was worthy of.

Home time.

162

Part VIII - The Path Less Trodden

Chapter 16

'Why me?' said Shug.

'You and Tiberius,' replied Ben.

'OK, *why Tiberius and me*. Why not someone from the military, or the CSN?'

'I have been through this for the last three days with the FDR, with FEPAC, and with the Elders, and we come back to the same conclusion time after time. No one from the military has the negotiating skills, or the scientific background to get or determine a solution, the scientists do not have the negotiating skills or the survival instincts to stay alive long enough to get or determine a solution, and as for the diplomats, they aren't equipped in *any* of the skills required for this journey, or any journey for that matter. You know that.'

Ben was being 'diplomatic' in his description of the Diplomats. What he really meant was they were a waste-of-space and it's safer to keep them 'occupied' in their ivory towers down in Parliament Square. Shug had no argument against his analysis of the military and the scientific community's skills to achieve such a task, in such a hostile environment and within such a tight timeline.

'Shit'!

'The two of you will be able to get as far North as the wastelands where the Traxons will be waiting to assist you on the final leg to rendezvous with the Dolphins. You know how inhospitable the wastelands can be. The Traxons are renowned for their hand-to-hand combat prowess, if anyone can give you a fighting chance of reaching your destination, they can.'

Trax is a walled city in the Northwest, almost impossible to reach as an impenetrable dank swamp and the quickest quicksand known to beast, or man, surround it. The Traxons were beaten and besieged for many years forcing them from their lands and had them forever retreating until all that is left is the walled city, and due to its altitude is known as Citta Alta - 'the high city'. They would have lost this also if they hadn't in the distant past formed an academy to train the young Traxons to be ferocious warriors. Yes, they are brilliant warriors but their most noteworthy talent is their ability to double-time it for hour-upon-hour, day-upon-day, through the densest jungle and across the bleakest terrain without fatigue. No one can stay with them on such occasions and this, the most fearsome tool of their arsenal, is phenomenally effective in times of war.

As a Race they are quiet and unassuming, almost shy, only ever venturing to the low lands for very special meetings of the Senate or to buy specialist materials or medicines that they can't manufacture or produce themselves. They are similar to the humans in form but smaller and wider, the tallest reaching maybe 5ft. The girth comes from the hard manual labour of maintaining the city and mining the minerals to sustain their economy, the fact that the Traxons were to join them for the most dangerous part of the quest inspired Shug.

* * *

Saying 'no' can upset people. It's better to let them down gently. Also, you need to say it three times. The first is met with unbelievable surprise. And shouting. A lot of shouting. At this point you may have to be more forceful – 'NO!' There are now threats to accompany the shouting. Some life threatening, some not. It's the third 'no' that secures the deal. You can feel good about this, because a successfully delivered 'no' is almost as good as receiving an indisputable 'yes'. Pat on the back.

With the break-down of the talks between Ben and Bob and Bob's government, war was inevitable. There was no way that the humans would halt the extraction of the quintyllium ore, which in turn, meant that many more haggii would die. They had already begun tunnelling in three of the nearest mountains to Ben Nevis, destroying the communities there. It was easy to see where they were headed – the Three Sisters, about a thousand miles north.

The Three Sisters; so called because it was a range of the three highest peaks in the land clustered within a one hundred mile radius. Magnificent. Menacing. Never looked the same two days in a row, or two hours in a row for that matter. The light changed, the clouds dispersed, clear skies and shards of sunlight broke through like mighty lasers puncturing some giant maelstrom in a faraway galaxy as it struck and reflected off of the wet rocks of the Sisters. This was completely breathtaking. Almost eerie. It wasn't well documented or reported that these mountains were the richest in quintyllium, the Haggii geologists having kept this secret over the years but unfortunately, the humans already suspected this. They were also the most populated of the entire nation. Losses would be heavy, *if,* nothing was done.

The only positive thing that Ben was able to secure from the talks was a cessation of mining for one week to permit the haggii to offer an alternative solution to the generation and production of oxygen that precluded the use of mass mining quintyllium.

'It's a tall order I agree, but our only hope,' whispered Ben.

Shug sat with his head in his hands. Tall order? He couldn't believe what he was hearing. Ben wanted him to consult with the Dolphins, in the Northern Territory. Across the wastelands of Trax, past the swamps of Argee, and to get to Argee he would have to penetrate the almost impenetrable jungle of Quadrafiernoble. What was Ben thinking about? 'Trust me, Shug, between you, *you* and Magdalena; I believe there's an answer to be had. Neither of you could ever do it alone, but between you… you'll be amazed what can be achieved.'

Shug was intrigued, Ben knew something he wasn't letting on, or, was he losing it? He had, after all, been under a lot of pressure in these last weeks. Was the pressure getting to him?

'Think about it, Shug. Quintylium *is* the answer, but is mining the ore pounding it to dust the most elegant way you can think of of extracting oxygen?' Shug shrugged his shoulders. Dumb answer, maybe, but he wanted Ben to give him a hint, a starter for ten if-you-like.

'Right listen. Think basics, back to early days of the Institute. A very basic way of changing the atomic number of quintyllium and adding the electrons needed to produce oxygen is to accelerate it to light speed in an atmosphere controlled accelerometer, maybe halogen or argon, collide the atoms against heavier atoms – say plutonium or uranium or the like, and what do you get?'

Shug hoped it was a rhetorical question.

'The humans are barking up the right tree', continued Ben, 'it can be done, but the fall-out will be catastrophic. Think about it – a radioactive element, say Quintyllium 235 or Plutonium 239 and adding an extra electron? How unstable can you get! We can't go around banging rocks together, the consequences are dire for all-of-us, you and me included in.'

'I need some time to consider this. Unless you can tell me what's on your mind, specifically, I'm uneasy about being the choice for this journey.'

'We don't have time, Shug, you're our only hope we have exhausted ever other avenue open to us. It's this, or war.' Ben wasn't pulling any punches, Shug could tell by the drawn look on his face. He let out a long sigh. 'OK, we'll set off at dawn, but Tiberius and I need the help of the Traxons to get through Argee, are you sure they will help us?'

'They have already agreed to meet you there in three days time, you know how dependable they are', said Ben.

'Thanks, you realise the humans will do anything to make sure we will fail?'

'I'm aware of that. Be careful. There are many of our allies between here and the Wastelands, they are all on alert and will be there to lend a hand. But consider this – Vibex has grown to dislike you and would love to see the initiative fail. He would stoop to any level. Your friendship with King Bob is the reason for the hatred.'

'What, is he afraid I'm going to steal his job?' laughed Shug. Ben didn't answer, but he could see by the look on his face he wasn't far off the mark. This was something else Shug could do without.

* * *

Shug thought of the journey that lay ahead through in his head as he prepared a few necessities to take with him; skian dhu, sword, body armour, hypersliders, energy capsules, water flagon. Food would have to be won along the way – they had to travel as light as possible.

He mentally planned the route ahead – exit Haggii City Central through the North West gates – up past race mountain towards St Icarus Bay. They'd have to circumnavigate the Bay to stay out of trouble, so would be heading east before doubling back onto the North-West Trail and into Trax. They'd come close to the Canyon of Fathomless Regret, but should be far enough west to avoid entering it – thank god! Then it was due north up the west coast to the jungle of Quad, through the Swamps of Argee into the wastelands and a final push onwards to the Oceans of Arctic to meet the Dolphins. Easy!

He would spend the dusk as usual paddling in Loch Lomness. He thought of the days ahead; hard, dangerous, sweaty. Fatigue would be a problem as the terrain was universally tough; maybe dehydration too, due to the exertion involved crossing this terrain with some areas almost desert. Mountain, river, jungle, swamp. Or was that murderous mountain, wretched river, jinxed jungle, and swarthy swamp? For sure there were dog days ahead!

Dog Days? Why dog days? Why was he thinking of perplexing questions on the eve of the hardest journey he was likely to take?

Can't help himself, that's why.

The loch wasn't just as flat as usual, a bit colder too. Large bow waves were breaking about a mile from the shores and reducing to not insignificant ripples as they buffeted against his legs in the shallows. Dusk today was ominous, as if nature knew the backbreaking toil and thunderous tribulation that was in the air. The sky was low enough to bathe the surrounding mountain peaks in a dense velvety mist.

Why not cat days or donkey days for instance? Everyone knows cats have an easy life; three snoozes a day before their long

174

rapid eye movement main snooze in the evening. Then getting up to prowl the streets in the wee early hours of the morning hunting imaginary vermin. They knew they didn't actually have to kill anything to eat to stay alive as they had as much food as they liked back at their owner's homes. No, cat days didn't really fill the phrase with realistic authenticity. Donkey days? A bit closer maybe as some of the donkeys Shug knew had a poor standard of living – low paid job, little or no thanks from their overbearing bosses, out-of-date carrots and turnip for their lunch, hay to sleep on which was way past it's sell by date, not to mention that their home lives, mostly, were a misery due to overbearing and demanding wives and girlfriends. Yes, donkey days could be a good way of describing tumultuous times. But dog days had a better ring to it. Dogs were always moaning and complaining about how hard it was being a dog. Although, come to peruse the matter, not all dogs were this way. Some breeds were very mild mannered and polite and never complained. In fact most breeds were like this, it was just the angry minority that stole the headlines with their incessant moaning and short-tempered sniping, the small yappy ones that would always chase you and try to bite your ankles. So should the saying be changed from dog days to donkey days? No didn't quite have the same impact. He became concerned, why were all dogs tarred with the same brush? Did the scholars in the early days get it wrong, or was he barking up the wrong tree? (Another pun like that and he'd be heading home with his tail between his legs)! Enough! That's it!..

He kicked the water, splished up and down a bit and tried to fathom the perplexing question. Did it mean bad days? Maybe dog days were in fact good days full of laughter and fun? Beginning to get further away from the mark, here. Further away from the mark? Reminded him of the joke – Q; what goes mark mark? A; a dog with a hair lip!

Why, for goodness sake, "dog days"?

He stared at the sky, the first stars of the night beginning to shine through. Sparkly, twinkly, spangly. Then, on the horizon he spotted, aptly enough, Sirius – the Dog Star. What was it the ancients discovered about Sirius?...., yes, at a certain time of year Sirius rose at the same time as the sun – and this was usually the harbinger of the hottest days of summer, *the overwhelmingly hottest days of summer*. Yes – the phrase didn't depict hard-times or mistreatment of dogs, it just meant that the particular day was particularly hot! Although Shug would accept and continue with the metaphor that could be taken here to describe the days ahead, seemed too good a fit for the challenge that was in front of him – more pertinent, it would turn out, than he could ever imagine.

Yesss! Shug had it!

Part IX – Why the Long Faces?

Chapter 17

It was a close shave. An Oraxonite hunting party had come within yards of where Shug and Tiberius had darted into the undergrowth to take cover, and no clues as to whom they were hunting; armed to the teeth they weren't out mogeling round the woods.

'What do you reckon?'

'Hard to say, fifty maybe fifty-five,' replied Tiberius.

Too many for the two of them, that was for sure. The thud, thud, thud, of heavy hooves on moist earth from the battalion on-a-pace through the jungle, had given them away, they could be heard from a mile off.

So why couldn't the pair of them take off at near ¾SofL and lose them? Well, it isn't that simple. The mountain you see, the racecourse or circuit if-you-like, is well marked-out and each racer knows it like that back of his, or her, hand. Every bump and hollow, every nook and cranny, mapped out in the racers mind to many decimal places. This allows them to have their mind and eyes a corner or two ahead of the corner their body is actually negotiating. Anticipation & peripheral vision; crucial tools of any racer, hence the very high speeds. In terrain like this, on the other hand, they were lucky to cover fifty miles in a day. This was the meanest, baddest jungle on the planet - Quadrifenoble.

'We need to keep moving, Tiberius, it's only a matter of time before they return or another hunting party comes across us. If we can get to the other side of St Icarus Bay at least the Traxons will help us in any scuffles.'

'Easy for you to say, said Tiberius, but how do you know that the Traxons are even going to help? Or, that the Dolphins can answer anything? I can't believe Ben talked you into this wild-goose-chase.'

'You can't believe me, what's got into *you*?'

* * *

Why chase Geese anyway? Shug had never chased a goose in his life, wild or otherwise. And, did they have to be wild? Wouldn't a tame one do, (be easier to catch, surely)? Would that take the fun out of it? Shug was wandering off in another perplexing question. Maybe the pressure was getting to him? He caught Tiberius' eye. Just a fleeting glance mind you, but enough to put a nagging doubt at the back of his mind. What was wrong with him? Was he imagining it? Tiberius, his best friend, (along with Hamish), formidable warrior, and brave racer turning against him turning against the Nation? No, never, he was havering. But there was that incident at the last forum of the council, when Tiberius had sided with the fanatics. Also, the incident in the final round of the world championship race when Tiberius ran him off the track – lost the race, and could have been killed. Yes; he wasn't himself of late.

'Are you listening?'
Shug shook himself back to the present, 'What?'
'If we split up we have a much better chance. You head North-West to rendezvous with the Dolphins, I'll head North-East and attempt to recruit the Hezmanni to the cause, we can meet at Loch Ness and head South together, in a much more formidable position.'
'When did we want to be formidable? The plan is to determine a method in which to produce oxygen artificially without reducing

our mountains to rubble. Don't go all fanatical on me at this stage.'

'The Oraxonites are out to stop us, by any means they wish, the humans almost certainly have rebel patrols in this area, looking for you know who, and Vibex would love to see you beaten. And dead.'

'I know exactly what Vibex wishes of me, but together we are stronger, divided we reduce our chances of success, exponentially!' Shug had had enough of Tiberius' ravings.

'I am continuing to the meeting with Magdalena. You do what you will, but understand the gravity of your actions'.

'I'll continue onwards to Hezmanomov and meet with you at Loch Ness. Trust me I know what I'm doing.'

And before you could say boo to a goose Tiberius disappeared into the jungle.

'Am I paranoid?' thought Shug, 'does he know something I don't?' He headed into the jungle in the opposite direction just as a shadow emerged from the undergrowth into the clearing they had just left. Vibex. Several more humans emerged from the shadows. Had they heard everything that was discussed? Vibex motioned for half of his men to follow Tiberius, and said to the others 'let's stop this before it starts!'

Shug had been travelling northwest for two days and two nights. Fast. Exhausted, sweating… bleeding, he needed to stop and rest and recharge, but was thinking; get to the other side of the Bay by nightfall the back of the journey would be broken. Or, was that Crusade?

St Icarus Bay? '*Damn*' – he sighed under his breath. Needed to cross the Bay. To circumnavigate would take too long, it'd be too late.

The Icaria are a close-knit barbaric race, almost insular, and don't take kindly to strangers, in a way that predators don't take kindly to predators! The pain and suffering of the lost souls who had inadvertently wandered into the Bay was legendary, creatures that had met terrible terrible deaths. To be Icarian is to be pitiless, to be ferocious, to be compassionless.

Crossing the bay now would be suicide, Vibex and the Oraxonites were closing in fast from the south, and in front the entire Icarian nation. What is needed is somewhere to hideout, a safe place until nightfall. The sun refracted violet through the early morning mist that hung in the air with a stench palpable enough to make strong Haggii weak. St Icarus Bay was beautiful but the water in the bay curdled red with the blood of the many who had been mercilessly and pointlessly slain. It was surrounded on three sides by the bleakest mountains on the planet, mountains that had never been conquered, *summits without flags*. Shug knew if he could get to a decent altitude on the mountains neither the

Icaria nor the Oraxonites could follow. Survival at such a level would be marginal, even for a haggis. Is it worth the risk?

'Talk about being caught between the Devil and the deep blue, I'll have to deal with both...'

He began the ascent of the range on the Bay's Southside travelling as quickly as was safe to do so. It was cold and getting colder.

High, higher, highest.

Judging by the density of the air must be about four miles above seabed level.

Pausing for breath he scanned the surroundings. This astonishing perpendicular landscape hit him like some kind of exciting colourful soundscape. Soundscape? Listening with his eyes? Colourful? Sight and sound were coalescing in this strange land of awesome verticality. He gasped and sighed thin.

'Need to find some shelter, won't survive two hours in these conditions.' The sweat that had covered his back turned into a nanolayer of frost burning like sulphuric acid. It was becoming ever surer that the earlier thought; 'is it worth the risk?,' would return to haunt him.

The wind that had picked up the newly fallen snow turning it to blizzard, died away.

An ominous distant rumble reverberated across the wet snow and off the wetter rock. Avalanche! Looking up, he estimated that if cover wasn't found in 20 seconds flat there'd be no coming back. About five hundred yards away a shelf of dislocated rock jutted out from the shear face of the mountain just enough to get his body under. He lunged for it.

It lasted about ten minutes, probably dislocating a million tonnes of snow and rock. And, his left shoulder. The shelf wasn't just as big as it first looked. With a swift bang the shoulder was relocated against the very shelf that failed to protect it. Grey slate! The swelling and bruising that follows such an injury would almost definitely render his arm useless for a few days.

Suddenly, and with more than mild surprise, straight in front was a small opening in the rock. Wasn't there before, must've been uncovered by the avalanche. Was it a cave? He moved towards it checking there was no more snow about to fall. It certainly was a cave. Quickly squeezing through the small opening only too aware that in a few minutes the swelling of his shoulder would almost certainly prevent access.

Inside, the cave was massive. He quickly pulled some rocks and snow across the opening and was sure that the Icaria or Oraxonites would never be able to get this far up the mountain but didn't wish to take any chances nevertheless. Exploring the cave threw-up some unexpected findings. For sure, someone lived here. Skins from all types of creatures were scattered around. Food too, well, it could be taken that the dead animal carcasses were killed to be eaten and not for sport. There were also hand made torches stacked in a corner with some flint for lighting them. He took one and kindled it into a warm orange glow. The faint glimmering revealed wall paintings of beautiful dexterity. Depictions of daily life; happiness and sadness, and famine and feast, war and peace and life and death and life. It was instantly recognisable that whoever lived here was civilised in the extreme.

Venturing further inside there was a massive underground lagoon, black as coal and glass mirror smooth. Ominous. Thirsty after the rapid ascent, the thin dry air had left his throat like sandpaper and at the far corner there was evidence of a ripple, followed by oxygen bubbling to the surface, the water was flowing so should be OK to drink? *'Never drink from a stagnant pool!'* He clasped his hands to scoop up some of the water and was astonished that it was warm. A hot spring at this height? A swift conversation with himself along the lines of:-

'No way?'

'WAY!'

convinced him entirely it was no mirage. Immediately taking the plunge, and swimming deep and long, the warm water brought life back to his freezing bruised limbs. He swam as deeply as possible without reaching the bottom. The pressure at that depth convinced him returning to the surface should be executed as gently as possible. Although the pressure was good for his shoulder, compacting the muscle and tissue and all, it wasn't any good for his eardrums and circulation. In fact, having swum around for so long, he wasn't sure in which direction the surface was. Letting a small amount of oxygen from his lungs, the bubbles formed travelled towards the surface showing the way.

He broke the surface of the lagoon with an almighty th'dwhooosh, gasping-in a massive amount of air and laughing like a maniac. He stopped mid-laugh. The lagoon was surrounded by about twenty Icaria, all of who were tooled-to-the-teeth and ready for business. A voice from behind commanded 'OUT!' Shug pulled himself from the water, tired from the swim and aching from the avalanche.

'OK, who's first?' he croaked.

'Shug,' the same voice continued, 'we are not here to confront you. We are not enemies, we wish to help.'

'But you *are* Icarian?'

'Yes and... let me explain. We have turned our backs on the Icaria of the Bay, follow a different set of principles and pray to a different God. The violence and the killing doesn't sit well with everyone, those of us who disagree left the Bay some time ago to live our lives here.'

A simplification of the facts? This Icarian went on to explain of the civil wars between the various factions of St Icarus Bay, and how after many years of blood-shed, atrocity, and tyranny the group left to live peacefully here high on the mountain. The leader's name, Shug later discovered, is Dani.

'I was unaware that you were able to survive at this altitude, breathe air so cold and thin?' asked Shug.

'We can't', replied Dani, 'we all carry one of these.'

She showed him a small metallic cylinder. 'This contains liquid oxygen at a hundred atmospheres. The air up here fatigues us and significantly reduces our resistance to viruses and microbes. A swift blast from this and we're back to normal and our immune system remains at a level that can fight off the worst of 'bugs.' Each container has enough oxygen for about a month... depending on how hard we are working.'

'Obviously,' offered Shug.

She passed the cylinder to him, and turning it over repeatedly in his hands, he savoured the tactile enjoyment to be had. It was an exquisite peace of Engineering, had almost no weight, 'machined from solid?'

'Forged, with a simple machining pass and some heat treatment to finish the process'.

'Molto-bene, beautiful. By-the-way how do you know my name? When I climbed from the water you addressed me as Shug.'

'News of your quest precedes you. Everyone on the mountain and in the Bay is expecting you… you're the talk of the town.'

He let out a deep sigh.

'As I see it,' continued Dani, you could use some help getting across the bay if you're ever to bring this journey to a conclusion.'

'Is that how you see it,' replied Shug, sarcastically. It wasn't like him, 'sorry – cold… tired… hungry… pissed-off.'

'Don't worry, anyone that has been through what you've been through in these last weeks, would be a little cranky. Why don't we get you're shoulder looked at, get some food inside you and rest you for a day-or-two? At least then, you'll have an evens chance of clearing the bay, say, in three nights time.'

Although not liking what he was hearing, losing so much time, it was easily his best chance. Getting into a scrape now would almost certainly end in defeat. He agreed with the Icarian, and once treated and nourished, was shown to a kind of inner chamber of the cave where rest, repair, and strength regain could be had ready for the next chapter.

On the way down the mountain, Dani confided that even Benjamin Augusts Haggis had his doubts of Shug being successful. 'Is that what he thinks?' asked Shug nonchalantly.

Dani didn't answer, knew it was a rhetorical question.

'In fact,' she carried on, 'no one fancies your chances of bringing the quest to a successful conclusion.'

'Oh,' sighed Shug.

'Except me,' she whispered.

The base of the mountain was only a quarter of a mile from the edge of the Icarian settlement. Guard towers, two hundred feet high were spaced evenly around the boundary, manned by the less malevolent Icaria waiting and hoping for someone or something to come too close to their boundaries so that they could return home from work that night with a 'now that was a kill' sense of satisfaction deep inside.

The skies were a deep indigo as the sun set and the moon rose, sheet and forked lightening blazing psychedelic shapes across the horizon a couple of miles off-shore. The rains had turned the ground to an ankle deep messy brown pulp.

Dani offered Shug some advice on crossing the Bay. 'Follow the City walls clockwise towards the sea and at the thirteenth tower you'll find a gateway into the city. This is the least guarded part of the walls and is only used by the city tradesmen and refuse collectors. The gates are automatic so you'll be able to get through behind one of the trucks as they go about their work. I will ensure a diversion at this end of the bay, which will keep the guards busy ensuring you enough time to get through. Once in the city, keep to the sewer footpaths. These travel north to south so by following these you will end on the North side and from there it's only one hundred miles onwards to Traxon. Good luck.'

Shug sprinted to the thirteenth tower, using the bush and shrub as cover. The Icarian tradesmen were going about their business as usual and would do so allnightlong. Behind him from the edge of the Bay came a resounding explosion. 'And so it begins?' Suddenly Icaria police and military were rushing towards the South-Side and the explosion. He was sure that Dani and the others would keep them busy for a couple of hours.

Dropping deftly through the gates and down onto the sewer bank he made swift progress across the city, only now and then having to dive for cover as Icarian patrols policing the dirty wet streets came into view. The open sewers of St Icarus Bay are known far and wide and are a talking point amongst sewage professionals everywhere. The pungent stench of this urban waste is infused in everything; buildings, pathways, roads, even clothing. Of high viscous texture the luminous green waste produces gases that can kill. Fluidised bed reactors reduces the influent to a toxicity level that can permit the lagooning of hundreds of tons of the stuff each night, which is then turned to harmless effluent by the millions of friendly little aerobic microbes let loose on it and finally it is harmlessly disposed of into the sea. The filtration system could do with improving as the smell was indescribable. Shug criss-crossed the sewer matrix heading West and North, doing well not to throw-up due to the reek, until finally as dawn broke he was on the opposite side of the city. 'Just need to get past the last of the guard towers now.'

Chapter 18

Shooughhhthudd! Shoougthhwackk! Almost instantaneously two perfect arrows hewed his sternum into two scalding halves the only thing holding the breastplate together was skin and sinewy tendon.

They had been waiting, stupid not to have sussed them. The pain was excruciating. No time to panic, no time to bleed; time to run. Where? Surrounded. Ambushed! He unsheathed his sword and skian dhu, and in ten nanoseconds took out three raging, hissing oraxonites, a couple of humans, and an Icarian soldier for good measure. Skian Dhu in left hand for scything and hacking, sword in right, chopping and stabbing. Why were humans and Icarian fighting together?

It was a moot point and now was not the time to debate it. They were coming from all directions, fifty or more, couldn't fight them all off? Tiring, he cleaved a couple of humans in half; clean. Two of the ugliest, fattest oraxonites he had ever seen surged forward, the hatred in their dim empty eyes burning through him. Spinning one hundred and eighty degrees, sweeping the legs from below the first, whilst, simultaneously, thrusting his skian dhu into the other's neck, just below the ear, right to the hilt. Crimson blood spurted hot and sticky, covering his left arm. The one on the ground, realising the sincerity of Shug's retaliation, got up and ran, as did a few others. Shug roared a few expletives after them, hated cowards. Adrenalin was at boiling point. Another arrow struck squarely between his shoulder blades brining him to his knees. Blows rained down on his torso and head from all directions. Sword and skian dhu swung in all directions, hitting and missing inthesame amounts. He drifted in and out of consciousness. Could swear he heard Tiberius's voice; 'don't kill him, we don't need another holier-than-thou martyr…..'

There's betrayal and *there's* betrayal. This was something else. Like being hit by a train, or a bolt of electric blue lightening, or like when you're dreaming; dreaming of falling, hitting the ground and being jolted awake. Just like that.

How could he do it? Tiberius? Surely no? Surely aye!

Best friends since they were kids. Shared everything. Confided always. Their highs were very high and their lows very low. It was a bond? Evidently not. Tiberius siding with the Oraxonites? If it's a dream, it's a very sick one!

He would never forget it. The sadness and the emptiness would be closer to his heart. Forever.

Chapter 19

It was tough and about to get tougher.

Chapter 20

Shug came-too in an unfamiliar place. It was hot. The beach was pebbly; stones shaped and polished by a ferocious sea over eons. It wasn't ferocious today, quite the opposite in fact. The water was crystal clear, the turquoise hue dappled with a zillion stars of glinting sunshine that hurt the eyes, or at least, Shug's eyes.

A ramshackle wooden bridge projected from the beach about a hundred yards into the sea, swaying gently in the wind, timbers quietly creaking as it did so. Maybe for fishing from? He passed out again, to wake a few days later with the Xynbeme at work licking his wounds and applying splints to his arms and legs. Many thought they were fictitious, the Xynbeme that is, the stuff of folklore and legend. This was the worst beating he had ever taken and for a split second wasn't sure he could continue, only a split second mind you. Had to continue, everyone depended on him finding the answer. *Everyone!* Doctor Daisey, master physician of the Xynbeme spoke softly. 'To be honest.....' Shug hated that, anyone that begins a sentence with 'to be honest...' deserves a swift poke in the eye. Maybe she was nervous or upset. She continued.... 'to be honest, we don't think you can go on. Not for at least ten weeks, three months, maybe.'
Shug was devastated.

'They've broken nearly every bone in your body. Many of your major organs are burst or split or infected, or burst and split and infected. They left you for dead, dumped you in the sea, and it's just… *blind luck* the currents carried you to be washed up on our beach. We need to get you back to Xynbugga; if you're to live.'

The pain was sincere. He passed out again.

Came-too with Xynbeme paramedics extracting arrow heads – straight through his broken body and out of his back, couldn't pull them backwards through the entry points due to the barbs, this would leave gaping holes - no, straight through and out the back. Aahrrghhh! Hadn't thought about the arrow that had found its target between his shoulder blades. This, following the same logic, would be extracted through his chest?

He drifted blindly into a disturbed semi-conscious limbo, dreaming of mind numbing anaesthetics and sublime variants of morphine. Sweating profusely.

Time passed.

'They didn't take your weapons,' a peaceful voice emanating from the corner shadows announced.

'They wouldn't dare.'

The owner of the voice walked into the light, crossing the hard stone floor to the cold slate bed where Shug had been placed to aid his healing. Later, he discovered, it was taken as read that the minerals within the slate, mined from the local mountains,

197

permeated the skin infusing bruised and torn muscle with extraordinary chemicals that rapidly rebuilt strength and movement. Some say it kept him on the light side of death's door.

An oraxonite warrior would have to be out of his tiny mind to take Shug's sword or skian dhu. They were unique. The sword he had painstakingly made himself from the purest quintyllium alloyed with the finest titanium. The exquisite handle was cast from an exact model of his clenched right hand ensuring a perfect grip on the weapon could be had at all times. There were no fine or expensive stones encrusted in the handle. In recent years weapon handles had become very ornate and it was an increasingly fashionable thing to do these days, but would and would always, detract from the weapon's singular purpose. His skian dhu, on the other hand, was an entirely different story. This was a gift from Ben, and at the time of giving it he had said; 'this is very special.' This was as animated as Ben got, never one to show his feelings, almost 'gushing with excitement,' Shug remembered thinking at the time. It was a work-of-art, and state-of-the-art. Hardened and tempered in the ice-cold blood of a thousand fallen warriors gave it properties of toughness and hardness never before achieved in any metallic component, and some say, powers from the other side. It had in the dim and distant past, allegedly, cleaved a diamond in two.

Chapter 21

There is a potion, an elixir if you like, mixed by the Xynbeme that has miraculous healing qualities. Or, is it just a myth? He asked Dr Daisey if she had heard of this.

'The best healer of all ills is time my young friend. Best to forget your quest, the game's over. Stay where you are, we'll look after you, heal your wounds and you can leave when your strength returns. Sit down the game's over'

Hundreds of thousands of Xynbeme live and breed in and around Xynbugga, in the Northwest. It is a pleasant place with temperate climates and beautiful scenery. The coast road is particularly spectacular, twisting and weaving along the mountain range's edge, smashed day in day out by the roiling waves of Dead Man's Ocean. Daisey had led the Xynbeme most of her adult life and had a strong following amongst the creatures of this great place. Her experience and knowledge are such that when she speaks you listen.

'No way!' croaked Shug. 'You don't understand. If I don't return within a week, six days now, the world will end, well, the Haggii's world anyway, have no illusions.'

'I know,' she said. 'The news of your quest is rife across the land, everyone from the lowlands to the wastelands knows what you need to do, and are on your side as a matter of fact.'

They fell into silence, Shug knew that she knew of the potion, and she knew that Shug knew that there was an answer that could let him continue.

'It's massively dangerous,' Daisey finally confided. 'And the payback is not insignificant.'

'Tell me more.'

'To my knowledge, it hasn't been used in a thousand years. Less than half the beings that have been envenomated have survived, many dying terrible agonising deaths.'

'Envenomated?'

'Yes', she continued, 'do you think this is some kind of simple love potion that you drink, an elixir?'

'Well…, yes!'

Daisey began to break it to him gently. 'The 'potion' can only be administered directly from the producers, the Kobrite. Their venom from a single bite forms complex matrices, some of which work to splice bones together, some to knit gashed skin and torn muscle.

The process will take you to hell and back. In fact, forget it the game's over.'

'It certainly isn't.'

Chapter 22

Shug entered the nest to be greeted by a carpet of seething serpents. He grasped the closest serpent by the throat, (or his best guess of the location of a serpents throat), and swiftly removed its head with a single cut, and placed it in his top left hand breast pocket, followed almost instantaneously by cutting off its rattler, placing this in his top right hand breast pocket. Why? Shug wondered too.

He hunched down onto his hunkers, waiting.

The wound from the serpents, Daisey had explained, appears bluish-pink in colour and swells to the size of a large apple. Sweating, vomiting, nausea and muscle cramps, an irregular heartbeat and convulsions are common. Blindness, seizure, and paralysis would follow in equal measures. The first matrix forms in a few hours, but the entire brace of matrices takes about twelve hours during which time you'll travel to the outer reaches of madness and to the jagged edge of despair. If you survive, the matrices will hold you together for about two to three weeks, depending on how hard you push your body, obviously. *This is…* Envenomation, and once infected, there's no turning back.

Trepidation. He continued to wait. Tense.

The floor is a slithering, pulsating mass, the smell stinging his eyes. Through the darkness, one serpent rises-up and looks him direct in the eye, its scaly head and needle slit yellow eyes narrowing as it weighs him up. Another head appears to his left, and then one on his right. From behind, two six-inch razor sharp fangs pierce through his neck crushing his spinal column and shearing his spinal chord. About six pints of venom are pumped into his body.

Shug died a hundred times in the two days that followed.

The beasts that got their sight back after three days considered themselves lucky! No one can pronounce the correct name for the venom these days, some sort of obscure Latin dialect; but today it is know as Electric Soup. And the payback? You have to sell your soul. During the time the matrices form a visitor comes calling with a 'proposal you can't refuse', which, if you do fail to accept and have gone this far, your dead anyway.

In one of the rare moments of consciousness Shug had listened to Daisey, 'the Hezmanni are en-route, should be here tomorrow, you have until then to consider the significance of what you're doing.'

'Or insignificance,' threw in Shug, before drifting away once more.

The night.......

The Hezmanni duly arrived with another crushing droplet of information. The picture was forming.

Shug had nightmares about it in the nights that followed. He knew many Hezmanni. He liked them. They were a noble race. Why, then, would they be trading in souls? Of course, they weren't, this was the gold droplet of information to which we refer. They were only the messengers. The traders were the Icarian. Shug couldn't believe it, or more accurately, he could. These guys made Arundlesprocketsphere seem like a Saint.

The Hezmanni left Shug with no illusions, that if he proceeded and met with the Icaria he would die a young haggis, minus a soul, obviously.

Shug thought of his family; mum and Janice. And then his friends, Hamish, Tiberius, Dr Jon, Big Bill, and of course his mentor; Benjamin. They would miss him, but would survive, live on. The old adage; 'Life Goes On', takes on a new meaning this morning.

The pain now was psychological as well as physical and could feel it in every nerve, muscle, and brain cell alltheway to the heart of his *soul*.

Xynbeme

Shug's favourite song was 'Into the Fray'.
It went like this………..

INTO THE FRAY

Into the fray, into the fire
This is my only desire
And if I'm to die this day
I do so with a glad heart.
My people are saved for sure
My homeland remains pure

Into the fray, into the fire
Fight to remain free of your quagmire
And if I'm to live this night
A life hard-won is a life that's right
Will work harder for this liberty
Will spit my last breath to remain free

Into the fray, into the fire
Rush headlong below the Saltire
And if you are to die this day
Angels will line your stairway
I will rejoice and I will weep
Because of you, life is sweet

Into the fray, into the fire
This is our only desire
And if we are to die this day
This is the gift you'll never betray
We know you'll revel in your time
Will forge a Nation to her prime
Into the fray, into the fire

Chapter 23

Xynbugga was a long way from the Northern Territory and the Dolphins. Daisey spoke of the hazards and low-lifes he would meet between here and there. 'The Traxons will be with you, but don't relax for a minute – the outer reaches of Trax are as dangerous as anywhere, the dogs have venom that would drop a BerriBerriHill elephant, the microbes kill slower and enjoy the long drawn out agony of the prey, and the Icaria are always on the prowl for a brawl.'

'Icaria that far North?'

'Yes – but this is the least of your worries, the Oraxonites will know that we rescued you and will be looking to run you down and finish the job. And then Strathspey and hell to look forward to. Don't rest, don't lose concentration, and don't draw breath. Keep-up with the Traxons, let them set-the-pace they are well capable of getting through Strathspey swiftly and safely. Head due North from there and straight through the Swamps – Vibex isn't stupid enough to follow you there…, but the Icaria might.'

'The Swamps of Argee? Are you kidding?'

She didn't answer didn't have too; by the look in her eyes he knew she was serious.

'The Traxons will be here shortly. Good luck.'

With a final long hard stare into his eyes she turned and galloped back to her City and her kin, turning only once to shout back 'STAY FROSTY!'

Shug was alone and felt alone. The dark veil of night had crept up unannounced making the whole prospect feel overwhelming. He dropped to his knees and waited the long wait.

The incredible thud thud thud of the Traxons in the distance closing at incredible speed broke through the still night air. Standing up just as they entered his clearing, he could feel the dread amongst them - how could they be nervous? The Traxons? No Way! They numbered a hundred or more. Excellent!

Nathaniel stepped forward hand outstretched to say hello. Shug shook his hand and nodded. Then, gesturing with a slight backward tilt of his head, commented 'do you think you brought enough warriors?'

'Wish I could spare more, but things have deteriorated in the last few days. The Oraxonites have besieged Citta Alta, Vibex and a battalion from the Lowlands are heading towards Strathspey as we speak intent on sending you straight to Hell, and the Swamps of Argee are inundated with Icaria. More warriors?'

'Jeezuss. I was only joking – one hundred Traxons could war-down any foe.'

'I'm not sure how safe Magdalena is either. I've sent a Legion on ahead to… well to…'

His voice tailed off and Shug suddenly grasped the seriousness of the situation and had to take the bull by the horns.

'Right. This is what we're gonna do. We can beat Vibex, we can beat the Oraxonites and we can beat the Icaria. They won't even enter the Swamps – no chance – Dani will help us, I know it's her own people but she and her Followers have separated from them and hates the savagery of the Icaria of the Bay more than anyofus. So… as I see it, we need to get word to Big Bill from BerriBerri Hill to get down to Citta Alta and win that battle – leaving only Vibex to contend with.'

'What about the dogs and the microbes?'

'We'll think about them when the time is right.'

'Time enough?'

'Exactly. Into the Fray!'

It was a long night, hard terrain, hard won miles, and harder thoughts pummelling in his head. Now was the time to be confident, to be self-assured, to be arrogant - no time for self doubt, negativity or low confidence. Knew instinctively everything was going to be all right, was gonna be Okay.

The morning light brought the Walled City of Trax onto the horizon. Magnificent place, but the dust clouds that looked very pretty infused with purples, pinks, and oranges belied the state of affairs. The battle had already begun.

Nathaniel signalled to his troops to head straight for the City and the battle. Shug raced to the front and stopped them in their tracks.

'Nathaniel, this is one battle we don't need. Think about it.'

'Our families are there, our friends – besieged! Dying...'

Shug grabbed him by the shoulders stared long and hard into his eyes, 'we need to keep going, get beyond this – Big Bill will be there soon, the warriors that you left can hold the City until then – we need to keep going. Trust me. Please?'

Nathaniel knew they couldn't get involved, but this didn't ease the pain in his heart. His warriors looked on desperately seeking an answer, seeking more than he could give. Until finally; 'we can get through to the Northern Territory and the Dolphins with about half of us – anyone who wishes to get back and defend their homes and families can leave – it's OK, we'll get Shug there somehow.'

A young Traxon warrior pushed to the front and said in a matter of fact way 'I am confident that Big Bill and the BerriBerriHill guys will do what needs to be done so I will support Shug to the end.'

A rumble ran round the group until finally, with nods of approval emanating Nathaniel said 'Strathspey then?'

No one left. Everyone continued, Shug was humbled beyond words.

They circumnavigated Trax in a large anticlockwise arc bringing them to the foothills of Strathspey. They slowed to jogging pace then to walking, formed in three columns. In the distance were Vibex' colours flying high.

Nathaniel shouted an order to his men – 'stay in line, hold your station – we're gonna March right up to them and straight past them.'

As they got nearer it became clear that they must number around ten thousand, – mostly human, but a few hundred Oraxonites thrown in for effect. Vibex was on his black charger, armoured to the teeth and looking serious.

If they attack it will be a massacre.

Again Nathaniel spoke authoritavely – 'All… all of you… holster your weapons… *holster* your weapons!'

They reached to about one hundred feet of the massed gathering. Vibex didn't move, didn't order the expected onslaught. What was going on?

'Right people… pick-it-up.' Shug and the Traxon warriors stepped the pace and continued out of Strathspey and onto the Great Northern Trail that would take them to Argee.

'That was ballsy Nathaniel, ballsy *and* stupid!'

'Vibex *is* stupid, but not that stupid. If he attacked, the political and social fall-out would end his career and dethrone Spitfire Bob. They know they have to be seen to give you the chance to resolve the issue, even though they are still mining – they need to be seen to do the right thing by you. *Relax!'*

The Great Northern Trail was a good road – smooth as a billiard table and well lit. They made good time covering the thousand miles between Strathspey and the Swamps in just under ten hours.

Shug had only ever read about the Swamps of Argee, and seen photographs, but nothing had prepared him for the intensity and stench of the place. Dead trees plunged upwards from the green slime that covered the ground to about four feet deep like a liquid carpet of pus filled revulsion that no beast or man should ever have to be exposed to.

Shug puked. Nathaniel laughed.

'Weak stomach my young friend… wait 'til we get into the depths… you'll so not love this place.'

Shug puked again – had never been so grossed out. Even the Kobrite nest seemed like a warm fluffy dwelling place compared to this. They waded on in. The pus was remarkably warm. 'Shit,' thought Shug, 'this is revolting – what about the microbes?'

Suddenly in the distance through the trees they could see a battle was in full flow – 'Christ… Icaria?' shouted Nathaniel.

'Don't know – Dani? We need to help.'

They charged as best they could, wading through the treacle-like swamp.

'Don't worry,' roared Nathaniel – the odds are even – everyone has to deal with this.

Shug plunged his sword deep into an Icarian's chest. Everything slowed down – everything was in slow motion. Looking around he was mesmerised by the ferocity of the Traxon onslaught and glad they were on his side. Dani rushed towards him stabbing down over his shoulder with her sword into the warrior behind him.

'Watch your back, Shug.'

'Thanks – back-to-back?'

'Let's dance!'

They turned back to back, each protecting the other from the murderous attack. They killed many. The Traxons killed more, until suddenly everything returned to normal speed, seconds became seconds again. Looking round they were amazed there was no one left to fight. How did that happen? It was over so quickly.

But, the price was high. Many young Traxons lay dead. The fires raged on, the stench of the swamp was diminished by the stench of death. Many of the wounded screamed in pain – broken bones, torn flesh, slowing heart rates en-route to flat-lining. The pride and glory of dieing in battle are, and will always be, illusory.

The survivors carried the dead and the wounded, through billows of smoke and raging fire, to the edges of the Swamp. Returning many times until the task was complete. Shug always thought that when you look into someone's eyes after a battle there is something different, something deeper, something that would never leave them, something they would have to live with the rest of their lives. A certain sorrow. This sorrow is compounded – battle upon battle, war upon war. It shouldn't be this way it doesn't have to be this way. He could never hold back the tears he shed for young Warriors slain in the heat of battle. Today was no different.

But, now wasn't the time to be getting melancholy, they had to keep going. Dani pushed Shug and Nathaniel and what was left of the battalion to continue into the Northern Territory to meet with Magdalena, they had to be strong enough and bold enough to continue, to put an end to this. She and the rest of her Icaria would tend to the wounded and bury the dead, including the Icaria of the Bay.

'Thanks, I'll never forget you.'

'It's all on your shoulders now, Shug. We have every faith in you. I've always had faith in you.'

Nathaniel and the Traxons waited patiently at the edge of the swamp until Shug and Dani said their good-byes.

Shug pulled himself from the swamp and ran to the Traxons 'What are you waiting for? Time to meet with a beautiful Dolphin I think.'

'Lead on Macduff!'

They set off at a ferocious pace – out of the god-forsaken place that is the Swamps of Argee and into the beautiful wilderness that is the Northern Territory.

Chapter 24

'Magdalena Magdolin I presume?'

'Shug, we meet at last. Beginning to think you were a figment of someone's over excited imagination thought you were never going to make it. Pleasant journey, *I presume*?'

She was making fun of Shug's opening, or just being innocently funny, a question that needed no answer, and continued 'You're a complete mess, I wish there was something we could do to ease the pain?'

Magdalena Magdolin, reputed to be the most beautiful creature on the planet? Jesus! Was her eyes mostly; piercing ocean blue, and a certain smile that had a depth beyond any of the Seven Seas. Her face was kind and young, whilst emanating knowledge and experience of someone twice her age. He'd never seen any creature more beautiful or enigmatic. Her skin was as smooth as Venetian glass and had twice the luminescence, or at least, seemed like it. Completely and utterly breathtaking – the myth was well founded.

'Don't worry about me, I'm just hoping the journey was worth it, that Ben was right, his faith in you to solve our problem?'

'All in good time, first we must clean your wounds and get you rested, *then* we can talk.'

Shug was taken to a place of decadence he had only ever read about. The dolphin's palace was renowned across worlds; walls gilded with silver and gold, precious stones decorating every cornice and buttress; midnight blue, sunburst orange, oceanesque turquoise, floors of Egyptian marble polished to within an inch of their lives – it was incredible.

The Dolphins had a breed of animal servants that looked after their every need and whim, and also, were their greatest protectors. The Carobs were humanesque in form, genteel of manner, and were dependable to the point of giving their life if it would save a dolphin. They were deaf and dumb, and communicated with senses that no other animal had, or rather, senses that no other animal still had the use of – some kind of telepathy or extra sensory perception, maybe?

He was shown to quarters that were opulent beyond taste although, given the journey so far, and the dank caves, stark cells, rickety shacks, inhospitable huts and dank caves, he had had to endure, a little luxury wouldn't go amiss! Thought of caves twice? – he liked caves! Called himself into check - the beings he met who dwelled in these simple places had massive empathy and made sure that they gleaned the most from such meagre skinflint prospects. These caves and shacks and huts are homes to these wonderful mammals – and who was he to judge anyway? His minimal one bed-roomed flat back at Haggii City Central was just as meagre and not nearly as homely.

He was bathed and cleaned, his wounds dressed, and then fed a feast fit for Kings; mostly finest vegetables and fruits, but with a spattering of fish and meat – prepared so that the sauces and marinades kicked in twice or three times after the initial bite to offer complex and mystifying flavours – it was just what the Doctor ordered.

That night, he slept on a bed of superlative Golden Eagle feathers and was covered by quilts of the finest Goose Down which provided a level almost of sensory depravation that left a feeling of being back in the womb. In the morning, shards of sunlight washed over him through the most beautiful stained glass windows that he hadn't even noticed the previous evening and was bathed in purples, greens and crimsons, as a deep heat ebbed through every aching muscle in his body.

Two Carobs arrived with a breakfast that was quite alarming in its magnitude. He was still full from the previous evening's supper!

'Strange,' thought Shug, they're supposed to be dumb, but I'm sure I can hear them speak. Looked on, but saw no movement of mouth or tongue; one asked the other – 'Do you think he can make it, do you think he's made of the right stuff?' To which the other, a young female, replied, 'I don't know – he's gotten this far, so that has to tell us something.'

'Do you two know I can hear you? Can you hear me?'

A little astonished, they replied in unison – 'not hearing – communicating.'

'I didn't know I could do this,' confessed Shug, 'I need to speak with Magdalena.'

He was taken along corridors, passageways, walkways, and up and down steps, ramps, and ladders to arrive at a place he imagined was the centre of the palace, and, on coming around a corner was enveloped in a vast space, dominated in the centre, by an expanse of water, that at a stretch, could be described as an Ocean.

There were many many dolphins at, what could only be assumed, 'play'. The noise was thunderous, as they dived, tumbled, leapt, and twisted, as many as one thousand airborne at any one time. A sudden hush fell over the place as the dolphins realised his presence. The waters emptied as he was led to the 'shore's' edge where Magdalena appeared and inquired to his well-being.

'You won't believe this, but I can communicate with the Carobobo! Amazing, don't you think?'

'Do you think for a minute that what I'm saying to you is audible?'

'Ehh?'

'It is one of your unique gifts, Shug, that's one of the reasons you were chosen for this journey.'

'I don't believe it, communicating telepathically with the Carobobo and Dolphins? When and how did I learn this?'

It is not something you learn to do, it is an innate ability you've always had, and as a matter of fact, it's not a new gift either but a very old one. All haggii have this ability, it's just that through the passage of time they have forgotten how to use it, you have forgotten to remember how to use it. But to business, we can discuss the merits of this at length when time is less pressing. Listen carefully. We have been experimenting, well, simulating, the powers of quintyllium – its ability to transform, change composition at an atomic level, become a completely different element, or theoretically, a completely new one.'

'What, like alchemy?' offered Shug.

'No,' responded Magdalena, a small chuckle forming – 'this is not for Druids, or Warlocks, this is Natural Philosophy, if it were biological it would be a metamorphosis, like the chameleon, for instance.'

Shug concentrated harder, his brow furrowing.

'Our simulations show, that at ¾SofL, quintyllium undergoes this metamorphosis, and with the right catalysts, can be transformed into almost any element, for instance hydrogen… or maybe, oxygen even? Do you catch my drift?'

'And? Go on! Talk to me about the catalysts?'

'That's the problem, my young friend. We don't know.'

'You don't know? What does that mean? What does it mean - you don't know?' She went onto explain at length the hardware, software, and firmware they had invented to be able to simulate Quintylium transformation at these speeds, along with the successes and failures, delight and despair, encountered along the way. Many talented Scientists, Engineers, and Technicians had been killed as the simulations progressed to elementary experiment and as elementary experiment progressed to full-blown accelerator testing. They had been studying the phenomenon for many years, long before Shug was even born.

'What we do know, is that at this speed, quintyllium has the ability to take on, or throw off, neutrons, electrons, positrons, or quarks. The control or ferocity of the reaction is beyond our learning at this time. You need to understand that this is at the very frontier of knowledge of this world. I have told you what I can – *you* need to piece together the rest of the puzzle, if you don't...'

Her voice tailed off, her eyes welled-up with tears of despair she bowed her head.

Shug knew that getting angry now was futile. He saw to the depths of her soul and knew she was hurting, knew she wished she could give him more information.

In many ways, it was up to him now.

If the Dolphins have only half the story, he knows someone who may have the other half – Nessie!

'Don't worry, dearest Magdalena, you have formulated the idea, and given me the confidence to take this all the way – to solve the puzzle, to rescue ourselves from ourselves. But now, I must head South, I have an important rendezvous with a very good friend of yours.'

'Nessie?'

'Spot on! How did you guess? Shouting 'see you later,' as he turned and galloped off towards the palace gates, out into the open planes, and south towards Loch Ness where hopefully, the missing link and the last piece of the jigsaw could be discovered.

Chapter 25

Shug had to cross the Canyon of Fathomless Regret to get to Loch Ness and Nessie. This was the biggest, deepest, baddest canyon on the planet.

Every kind of poisonous amphibian you can name inhabits it, the water running through it is as deep as any of the Oceans and twice as cold with under currents and eddies that could rip your legs off, which was irrelevant really, as toxicity levels would kill any mammal in minutes, well, maybe not something as big as the

BerriBerriHill elephants but, saying that, they'd have only a slim chance of survival.

Shug was making good time along the jagged Northern edge of the Canyon looking for a suitable crossing point. 'Suitable?' that was a laugh; he knew it was the most dangerous 'A to B' journey anyone was likely to take.

Galloping along a dusty single-track path, he was about to stop for breath, when the track suddenly fell away, almost vertically. Pulling up as quickly as was hagganly possible, but not quick enough – head over heels down the thorny wet slope, arriving in a bruised and scratched tangled mess at the bottom in a pool of soaking clay blood and sweat, with the strangest looking three creatures he'd ever seen staring bemusedly at him. Neither man nor beast, plant nor vegetable, they seemed to have elements of all. 'What are you,' roared Shug in his gruffest of gravelly voices in a vain attempt to frighten them more that they were frightening him.

'It's not what we are, it's what we can do.'

That's strange, thought Shug, 'why are you speaking like that?'

'Like what?'

'Well the three of you, speaking a piece of the sentence each, everything broken into verbs, nouns, adjectives....'

'We don't know what you mean, young Haggis.'

'Oh,' said Shug, embarrassed. 'Don't worry, it doesn't matter, go on, what's that you were preaching; "it's not what we are, more what we can do"?'

It took the three of them to speak a spangly, jaggy, broken dialect, which was a higeltypigelty mix of English, Kanji, Gaelic, what-have-you, where one would speak **nouns**, another **verbs**, and the last **adjectives**. Proverbs, pronouns, and adverbs were not exactly out of the question, but were used in the wrong places and out of context, mostly. On closer inspection, he noticed that they were conjoined triplets, and after a few hours with them learned that they could never think as triplets, as two would always gang up on the third, that is, there was always one of them in the 'proverbial' barrel. They had their own wee blame culture happening, which was primarily down to; farting, burping, smelly breath, bad personal hygiene, etc. Physically, they could have been humans that had additional 'bits and pieces' added. Bits like – fins, gills, hooves, branches, roots, leaves, tails, and claws, even pieces of fruit were growing from their ample torso, or what could reasonably be considered the torso.

He would learn more of their origins later, but understood this was a cruel punishment to three of the most beautiful human sisters on the planet that had at one time betrayed an old 'friend' of Shugs, and hence, been transformed into the sorry creature that stood before him by one of the world's most talented Hexophirers, (a being with the power to metamorphosise any animate object into any other, or a combination of several), and in doing so, it was rumored that he had also given them the gift of second sight and hence as time passed they had become know as the Three Sages. It would be a while before the penny dropped and Shug would realise to whom he had bumped into.

'Friends of yours have forewarned us of your coming,' they explained, 'you should be grateful, you're lucky to be alive you should be dead; many times over a cadaver.'

In unison they started a bizarre incantation;

A ghost – just another mass within the void
Takes your glance and reverberates it aloud
But with the Haggis even your sternest gaze
Is absorbed, lost, can never outwit or faze.

'So what's that meant to mean, then?

'What does it mean? Exactly what it says! You have to listen young haggis… *lliiisten!*'

Shug raised a bushy eyebrow, '*Eh?*'

Cool & dark, a quietroom where walls advance
You live with rage - rage in silence
Sheets soaking wet, drums pummeling in your head
Can't recall, in the morning light, what the voices said.

'Oh, that's cleared things up then! Crystal!'

'Don't get smart young haggis, it's yours for the taking, the world's your oyster.' 'Listen, listen with your mind, and break out of the mould.'

'I don't believe it,' thought Shug, 'stuck in the middle of the densest jungle imaginable, there's a canyon forty miles wide full of creatures who wish to eat me alive, and you three havering on about quietrooms and ghosts. Sorry ladies, I have to get going:- no time to waste, need to get out of here, offski, skeedaddle. See you later, alligators.' And without further ado, picked himself up, brushed himself down, and was about to get some serious speed under his quintyllium shoed hooves when they started going off-on-one again;

> Wily and tranquilly she engages your glance
> Concealed in depths until that perfect instance
> When she'll play it over in her mind's eye
> In that sublimely brooding way she's realised.

'Sublimely brooding? Steady! You really need to get out more. But, saying that, you've almost got an iambic pentameter going there, carry-on.'

'It's you who are removed from reality, young friend, all your life actually. Wake up, grow, breathe, live!'

'Oh, that's fine then,' he said sardonically, 'sounds easy enough – run it by me ♪*One.... More.... Time?*'

> Rushing back from oblivion trancelike eyes
> Reflect you squarely - no place to hide
> Within the glacieresque sapphires to her soul
> You're frozen-in-time; another prehistoric soul

'Rushing Back from Oblivion – you plagiarists, I'm always rushing back from oblivion!'

'The she we refer to could be the Dolphin, or the monster of the Loch, maybe? And, just how old do you think you are?'

'Magdalena, Nessie? If your only skill is speaking in rhyme & verse continue so that I may decipher your limericks, continue please. And anyway, how would you know of Magdalena and Nessie, and, what's my age got to do with anything?'

They elegantly deflected his question and said in unison; 'Come with us, you can't cross until nightfall, to attempt to do so would be foolish and futile. With us, you have a slim chance of getting to the other side in relative safety.'

'Relative? What about Dan Dan the FerryMan?'

'Can you afford him? This is of whom we speak, but he only dares cross at night. Cordial introductions can happen later, but first, you must accompany us to shelter where you can eat and rest and solve the puzzle we have been commanded to deliver. Time to put-up or shut-up.'

'Understood.'

They led him to a small dwelling place that was remarkably homely. Constructed from oak trunks it sat in a leafy glen not far from the water's edge. It stood two stories high, and as he discovered later has another storey below ground level – a laboratory where the Sages worked feverishly dayindayout desperately trying to find a 'cure' to the Hexophirers curse.

The living area had fluffy cushions scattered around and over the varnished oak floorboards, minimalist furniture gave the place a very uncluttered feel, the moonlight white walls instilled a soft brightness, and the open coal fire gave it an emberesque warmth – he liked the place immediately, 'yeah, I could live here,' he thought.

The sisters hurried toandfro, spoiling Shug as if they were his own siblings – wine, fruit, and his favourite savoury snacks – it was like being back at his parent's house with mum and Janice going over-the-top in making him feel at home, in the hope that he'd stay "just a little longer" this time.

He never did.

Chapter 26

'So, who "forewarned" you of my coming,' Shug asked nonchalantly.

'Just when we're getting to know each other, you go and spoil it by becoming all business like again – *relax*, when was the last time you had a pleasant evening, worrying about nothing? Let us get you fed and watered and cleaned, then we can talk 'til the cows come home.'

They had a brilliant evening, the Three Sages regaling him with enchanting stories of the many disparate beings that had passed here over the years and the adventures that they had shared. And, although they were in hysterics most of the evening, Shug couldn't help but sense a certain melancholy and poignant aura in the room – after all, the sisters were trapped in this diabolical vessel of a body trying so hard to escape. He wondered how long it had been, but knew that now, was not the time or place for such a heartless question, regardless of the fact that it was a genuine question and would come from a good place. He pitied them and knew he shouldn't – and, at that moment promised himself to return here some day to check on their progress, or better still, would pay a certain callous Hexophirer an unsolicited, and probably not too passive, visit.

Suddenly, in the middle of telling his favourite gag – "Uncle Roger, Master of Wit and Ready Repartee", the three Sages looked at each other, nodded and turned to Shug, one holding her hand high palm outwards telling him or rather commanding him, to stop. Shame, was just at the part when the Clown's car exploded and he was impersonating the trumpet player in full flow, belting out 'When the Saints....' It's a great gag, guaranteed to bring the house down.

'What? Stop now, are you kidding me?'

'Time to go young Haggis. It's late, he's waiting,'

'Time is fleeting...' whispered Shug.

The sisters covered him in a black metallic cloak – a strange material which Shug stroked between fore finger and thumb. 'Liquid Inconel?'

'S'shh, don't take this off until you're well beyond the Canyon's edge – it's to protect you from the grief this place exudes, it's not called the Canyon of Fathomless Regret for nothing.'

Dan Dan the FerryMan was at the waters edge. He looked a bit too stereotypical of the classic fantasy novel Ferryman – a bit too much like the grim reaper. Shug tried to break the ice – 'have you ever worked on the river Styx?' The three sisters caught his eye and with a singular look conveyed that this question was like asking a Turkish musician to play 'Zorba the Greek!' So much for breaking the ice! Dan Dan beckoned with a skeletal hand – Shug, knowing the seriousness of the crossing stepped onto the Gondola shaped boat, handing over the single gold piece the sisters had given him, along with a strange shaped object, metallic certainly, and due to its weight or lack of, a very exotic material. Shug imagined that it was a quarter of something much larger – and thought - if reflected about a horizontal plane and again about a vertical plain, it would become a perfect dodecahedron. Strange, but no time now to analyse the situation – had to get to the opposite bank.

'You can tell us about Uncle Roger next time.'

The trip would take about two hours and Shug wondered what wonderfully toxic ingredients the Sisters had distilled in their exotic cocktails they had been feeding him the night before. His throbbing head was pounding and his tired eyes blurry. 'Need a hair of the dog,' he quietly thought as the boat silently bobbed and weaved to-and-fro.

Hair-of-the-Dog? Where does that come from? He needed an electric-blue loch and a sublime dusk to contemplate this perplexing question. Or does he? 'Daniel, where does the saying hair-of-the-dog come from?' Dan Dan the Ferry Man looked towards him from under his hood and didn't need to say anything to get his message across.

'On my own then,' thought Shug. Well, dog and hair couldn't be taken in their literal sense, as neither are liquid and therefore can't be drunk. Must be metaphor for something deeper. Could it be Hare of the dog, that is a hare that, say, a greyhound may have caught and slaughtered and the blood was to be consumed to relieve the symptoms of the previous evenings frivolity? Maybe? Didn't fancy testing the theory 'though!

What about a blender? You could shave the hair off the dog and blend it to a liquid to drink and maybe relieve the symptoms? Stupid! Not remotely convincing. Dog, or dogs were sometimes referred to as the gear mechanism for selecting different gears internally in a gearbox. Could it be you had to drink heavy gearbox oil to be cured? Closer with the blender or dissected hare, here. 'I'm getting nowhere with this!'

'It's to do with the hair of the dog that bit you,' piped up Dan Dan. 'Hmmm,' pondered Shug. Trawling back into the dark mists of his long-term memory, he could vaguely remember a custom the Xynbeme practised, where if one of them was bitten by a mad dog, they used to stitch up the wound using hair from the tail of the dog to cure the wound. And it had to be the same mad dog or it wouldn't work the saying went. Ah! So it's nothing to do with alcohol it *is* used metaphorically and an analogy to cure a hangover by drinking the same drink as the night before to numb the effects!

Yessss! Shug had it!

Part X – PutUporShutUp

Chapter 27

It was mid morning by the time he descended on Loch Ness, a strange hazy morning, pleasant thoughts of the bizarre creatures that had lined the route between the Dolphins and here percolating through his mind. Everything was very still very quiet, the Sun set low in the Autumn sky casting long shadows across the water which as always was mirror like; inky black, not a ripple. The banks are composed of peat, which over the years has dyed the water black adding credence to the unholy Monster stories.

Shug needed to get to the opposite bank where he knew there was a discrete vantage point from which a view of the entire Loch could be had in relative safety and more importantly, a humungous horn to summon Nessie, (who's being discreet now)? There he could wait upon her arrival. Pausing for a moment taking in the fantastic sight of the loch encircled by the magnificent snow capped mountains before wading into the water, which was colder that usual making him gasp as he submerged up past his shoulders, then with powerful strokes, hauled himself into the placid icy depths.

About half way across he came upon a hullabaloo of Water-Buffalo splishing, sploshing, squishing, and skooshing their way up the loch. Couldn't believe it – wrong time of year for a start and at *this time* of day? The Water-Buffalos are notorious for having massive swimming parties where they will swim from one end of a loch to the other with the usual boisterous behaviour and buffoonery inbetween, not to mention the copious amounts of alcohol consumed along the way. Dangerous? Maybe a little, but Shug had never heard of any buffalo being injured in all the years he was acquainted with them.

He had two choices; wait for them to pass, which could take a couple of hours, or swim down the loch and round behind them coming back up the banks of the other side – again a good two hours in anyone's book. 'Damn!' Going under them, although probably the quickest way, was out of the question. Imagine; the legs of four thousand water-buffalo, that's sixteen thousand legs, pummelling the water furiously to keep their massive bulk afloat and the eddies and undercurrents that that produces - it would be suicidal.

Suddenly a voice form behind shouted – 'hey shithead, what you doing doggy paddling around here?' Shug, went to amber and turned in the direction of the booming banter. 'Wait a minute; I thought I recognised that *squeaky* voice – Smiling Jack Water-Buffalo, how the devil are you?' Jack played in one of Shug's old bands and they had kept in touch after 'musical differences' had ushered them on their merry separate ways. Jack had a great set of teeth, cost him a lot of money, hence the nickname Smiling Jack, even when he was down or feeling under the weather he couldn't help beaming from ear-to-ear getting every penny's worth.

'I'm fine, but by all intents and purposes, you look as if you could do with some help. Are you lost? Have you been beaten?'

Shug must have looked as bad as he felt. 'It's a long story – but forget that, Nessie will do her nut if she catches you lot in here; you know that?'

'Nessie? It's just myth, a legend; you don't think we believe those old haverings do you?'

'Don't say I haven't warned you!! Hey I need some help – you and your pals couldn't open up a channel and let me through, could you? It's not a big deal is it? I really need to get to the other side.'

'Are you serious? It's Queen Lala's birthday – only *the* number one event in our calendar – think, for instance, about you lot finishing a Hogmanay party early – it's that big a deal - HELLO!'

'Shit!' How could he not have remembered?, it's such a colossal event for the Water-Buffalo – their Queen is widely recognised as the favourite ruler of any Nation, (the antithesis of Eric of the Oraxonites if you like).

'Sorry Jack – I didn't even think – I'll get down loch and round behind you.'

'Hold on a minute Shug.' And with a grunt, a groan, and a guffaw, Jack was joined by six other Buffalo, who got under Shug and lifted him clear of the water, and before he knew what was happening was body surfing across the heads backs and shoulders of four thousand water buffalo to be dumped unceremoniously on the right side of them to reach his destination – thwooosh!!! He surfaced, swept back his mane and waved back across the loch to Smiling Jack and his pals before hauling himself to the bank in a little under an hour, not a record, but not bad for a soul carrying the injuries he has.

He settled on the grass surveying the mass of water in front of him. Loch Ness is about a hundred miles long, and fifty miles wide and is the largest body of fresh water in the land. The sun was higher and blazing brutally now, but having no effect on the mirroresque black water. Then the wind picked up, and there were no ripples washing from the south bank to the north – eerie! Picking up the brass-bronze alloyed double megaphone horn and ingesting as much air as possible he let rip with single blow. The reaction nearly blew him onto his back, his calves straining to keep him upright. The noise was deafening, easily 160decibels and the stillness that had settled over the loch was disturbed for the day, entirely, as all kinds of animals and birds were roused from the daily leisure of mogelling around the woods and launched themselves down overgrown paths or rushed headlong into the air disregarding the danger of being disembowelled by a Raptor or three.

It hadn't been long until up the loch, maybe a couple of miles, he spotted a tail fin slivery-slicing through the water heading in his direction.

Emerging from the water, she gave herself a good shake, her fur and scales matted to her body making her look very skinny, frail even. As she dried, the sheen of her feral cat like fur cast a satin afterglow, which contrasted brilliantly with the chrome like radiance of her scales.

'How old are you now Nessie?'

'Young haggis *never, ever* ask a lady her age, it's most rude!'

Shug didn't know her exact age, but did know, she was prehistoric, and *that's* old. Still looked great 'though.

'Prehistoric?' What was it the three Sages said about prehistoric? Glacieresque sapphires of her soul? To her soul? Frozen in time?

'You're looking a bit peelywally Shug, have you been in a fight? It's been a long time, why haven't you visited?, you know it gets lonely round here.'

'Sorry, Nessie, been busy – business is booming, I'm racing most weekends, gigging most nights – time is tenuous, you know that.'

'Tell me about it! Anyway – to business; you met with Magdalena Magdolin? How is she? Did she mention me?'

'It was an honour – she is truly the most beautiful creature in the land… along with you of course.'

'Of course…, ahmm.'

'She has a certain gravitas that is authoritative whilst being strangely soothing – do you know what I mean? We talked for hours – her palace is mind boggling, as is the loyalty of the Carabobo.

'Yes, I've been there many times – what did you think of the food?'

'Delicious – the hospitality is probably the best I've ever encountered – and I recall thinking; about time I had a decent break on this journey, too much toil and strife isn't good for anyone.'

'What about your dilemma?'

'Yes. She gave me a few pointers, but nothing that could be called the solution, danced around the periphery actually. Did say 'though, ¾SofL and Quintyllium are the key – talked a bit about catalysts and reactions. What do you think?'

'I've been working with the Dolphins on this for many years. Our simulations have shown that this is the way forward, but all we have is theory after theory and simulation after simulation; no one has attempted the quintyllium/oxygen experiment physically.'

'Guess that's what I'm here for?' said Shug, almost apologetically.

'It has been done, you know?'

'What?'

'¾SofL, of course.'

'You're kidding – the Elders said it was impossible, that "young Haggii have no place travelling at these speeds", they said it was impossible!'

'Listen Shug, let me explain a few of the more subtle facts of life. Ben has broken the barrier several times – many years ago granted, - but he's been there and back again. As have a few others, although these days it is frowned upon I agree, but it can be done, having said that – the barrier is the least of your problems. We can accelerate atoms to these speeds, but that's easy relatively speaking, they have zero mass or as close as damn it, whereas what we're asking you to do is accelerate yourself beyond this, yourself and a considerable amount of quintyllium through a void and into some kind of catalyst. We don't really have much of a handle on it yet. Mass, velocity, momentum!'

Again, the words of the Sages came back to him – "A ghost, another mass within the void?"

'Why is ¾SofL frowned upon?'

The stunned silence passed with no answer forthcoming until Shug finally said – 'you want me to get quintyllium to near light speeds, pass through some kind of "catalyst" that you don't really have much of a handle on and the end product will be the generation of oxygen on a planetary scale?

'More or less', she replied shrugging her shoulders in a mock 'easy-peasy' kind of gesture, 'but, seriously, we're 99% sure that this can be achieved, there are however a few caveats – well one, probably, well…, mainly.'

'Which is?'

'You're likely to be killed in the process.'

Shug let out a should-have-known-better kind of sigh, knew this was coming since the day he embarked on this remarkable journey – the creatures he's met, beatings he's taken, the lands he's surveyed… wouldn't have missed it for the world!

'Remember you used to say to me, my dearest Nessie, when I was very very young, it's not the critic; the being who belittles another's effort, no - the glory lies with the beast in the arena, the creature on the stage, the doer of the deeds, the protagonist – it is he upon whom the glory should be bestowed. Do you remember that? Well I've always been a doer, the protagonist, the beast in the arena. Glory? - The power and the glory never hurt anybody. I'll *see you* later.'

'Not if I see you first! And bytheway, ask Ben about Halogen.'

Chapter 28

Although desperate to get home, he sent a message back to Ben and Calculus asking them to meet him at the Edenite Collider – they had some work to do, couldn't return to the mean streets of Haggii City Central just yet.

Halogen, halogen... halogen – the word kept running through his head. If fluid dynamics was the key, he needed some sound advice this wasn't his bag so would need help calculating the mass, flow, pressure, temperature, and velocity needed to introduce the catalyst into the quintyllium's path – well, *his* path.

There was only one linear accelerator that could realise the plan. How big does it have to be? The Superconducting Supercollider of Eden. The Edenites were the designers, builders, and guardians of this colossal structure. The reasons to why it was built, and when it was built, had long ago drifted into legend, the question of 'why it was built' had in recent history become a moot point.

The developed length was just shy of two million miles, (the sun's ninety-two million miles away)! The materials of construction were most probably metallic, but certainly didn't coincide with anything on the periodic table. Even by today's standards the craftsmanship employed in the assembly of the superstructure was breathtaking. It was awesome. It could be viewed from afar on Table-Top Mountain, (so called because although the North, South, East, and West faces were shear vertical, the summit was as flat as the proverbial billiard table and stretched for miles). The collider was very slightly oval in section, with the major axis measuring about twenty feet vertically and the minor axis horizontal and measuring around nineteen; this helped the particles to be accelerated reach otherwise unobtainable speeds apparently, Shug did never suss out the mathematics of this geometrical phenomenon. From the mountain you could see one 'corner' of the structure that stretched one hundred miles east and one hundred miles south before disappearing below ground at each horizon. Although the plan view shape was circular, it also followed the curvature of the planet and stretched to about seventy five per cent of the spherical surface around 2000ft below ground, (see sketch). This was supermassive huge. Must have taken hundreds of years to construct. On approaching the gates he could see a few of the Edenites ambling around, and Ben and Calculus pacing to-and-fro impatiently. They looked nervous. An Edenite approached the three of them and with a motion of the head beckoned them to follow him. Or maybe her.

Shug had never seen a being of Eden before, but was pretty sure this was it. The story had it that they left the planet on completion of the collider and were only ever seen on their frequent visits to undertake maintenance tasks and had never been seen before the collider was constructed, incidentally. They looked human, but were different – very different in fact. Shug couldn't quite put his finger on it but the aura was wrong, amiss, not right. Their skin was white, not white pale as in when you're feeling ill… no… white white, but this wasn't it – there was something else. He couldn't explain it.

'Don't try to explain it,' said Ben smugly, 'just accept it, you'll never fathom the conundrum.'

They were ushered into a building that housed the finish and the start of the collider. The 'nerve centre.' In the control room they were instructed to 'don't touch nothing,' in no uncertain tones. The walls held bank upon bank of computer – to a level of excellence that Shug had only ever read about. The systems were updated frequently to remain State-of-the-Art. The Edenites are awesome technocrats.

The 'host' begun to explain; 'although this was designed to accelerate a given mass to light speeds, it has never done so. Not tested or validated. Only nanoesque atoms have been around and between the walls of the RudeTube and only to ¾SofL, no quicker. Also, it has lay dormant for over a million years, as we thought it would, so needs extensive shake down tests before it can be used-in-anger.'

'Why build it then? Why not wait 'till it was needed?' enquired Shug.

'Sshhh!' hissed Calculus.

The Edenite continued, 'although it has been maintained regularly it will take a few days before we are ready to attempt trial runs and get a handle on how big the job is to get it back to a condition where we can support Magdalena's request in relative safety.'

'Relative safety!' blurted out Shug, 'we all know that this is as dangerous as it gets, so lets cut the stalling and *get on with it*!'

'Shug, cool your jets' said Ben, 'it will take that amount of time for us to carry-out our designs, finish our calc's, and start having the components manufactured required to retrofit the collider for the introduction of halogen.'

'That reminds me…, tell me what you know about halogen, Ben.'

'Think about it, halogen is the only element we can introduce into the quintyllium's path to purify it enough to ensure the creation of oxygen is possible – you know that with quintyllium being neither organic nor inorganic – this is the only method of purification.'

'And getting it past ¾SofL, of course?'

'Of course – I forgot that wee bit. Let's get to work!'

They spent the next three days and nights designing the injectors for the halogen, sizing the vacuum pumps to pull enough negative pressure inside the collider to get the halogen to work, and to position and generate enough power in the heat pumps to introduce the thermal conditions for the reaction to crystallize. "They" meaning Calculus and Shug, Ben spent those few days in a corner sketching furiously and tearing up as many drawings as he created in the process. What was he doing?

On the morning of the fourth day, the three of them collapsed onto large sofas in an antechamber – finished – ready to go! 'I'm starving,' said Shug 'is there anything to eat around here?'

'Me too,' threw in Calculus – I need a shower first, and about three hundred years sleep!'

'Food? Sleep? How can you two think of such things in days like these?' Ben never was one for the necessities of life, continuing in a somewhat bizarre, for him anyway, upbeatmood - 'forget the food, let's see what you've done ladies, let's see your work.'

The light humour was a welcome break to the intensity that had enveloped the three of them these last few days but Shug couldn't help feeling a subtle sense of dread in their idle musings.

Ben lifted and surveyed the drawings and calculation sheets Calculus and Shug had completed. A few harrumphs, mucus clearings of the throat, rueful smiles, sharp intakes of breath through clenched teeth, husky coughs, and feigned heart attacks later, he turned to them smiling and said 'not too shabby – *not to shabby at all!*'

It was only the second time Shug had heard or seen Benjamin Augustus Haggis 'gush' like that. 'Eh?' The true master of playing it close to his chest was losing his rep'.

'Yeah, yeah,' said Calculus, 'and what have you been wasting your time on my old pal, are you going to show us your kindergarten sketches?'

'Time Enough Sir – let me explain what I was doing before I show you the design solution to a problem as big as the oxygen problem.'

'There-is-*noooo*-problem-as-big-as-*the*-oxygen-problem,' said Shug slowly and metronomically.

Ben shook his head before going onto explain that as the reaction took place in a vacuum at hugely elevated temperatures, and although water would form and evaporate almost instantaneously from the impact speed and pressure of the quintyllium on halogen, oxygen would take several hours to generate from the breakdown and decomposition of the quintyllium, and therefore, Shug would be in the most 'inhospitable' place in the Universe for the duration. In short – 'you'll be dead in nanoseconds… do you get my drift young haggis?'

'Good point, well made,' responded Shug sheepishly – 'what do you have?'

'Here, have a look at these.' Ben handed over a set of drawings showing a complex series of mechanisms and devices that would decelerate Shug from near light speeds, partition him from the ferocious reactions taking place behind him, inhibit the negative pressures that would see him EXPLODE, *and*, shield him from the three thousand degree temperatures that the heat pumps would introduce that could melt even an Oraxonites heart, (if they had one).

Shug and Calculus looked at the drawings in awe. Ben was infamous for his design skill and was widely held as *the* master of Master Draughtsmen, but the detail, accuracy, and passion in these designs defied belief.

'You didn't do this in the last three days… *did you?*'

Ben couldn't take a compliment and only answered with a 'well, this is the first time I've put pencil to film, but the ideas have been in my head since you took off on your vacation to see Magdalena Magdolin and Nessie!'

'*Vacation!??!!*'

Chapter 29

He had had a long and arduous journey. He was back. The answer was his.

It was the wee small hours when he crossed the borough boundaries of Haggii City Central, and knew instinctively this dirty old town would have a place in his heart forever – the good the bad and the indifferent as thousands of memories flashed through his mind; the good times and the hard times. Even in the pouring rain it emanated a tranquil beauty, the soaking wet streets glistening indigo under the purple afterglow of the ghostly streetlamps. It was quiet – no traffic, no revellers, no neon. Not a soul stirred – his hooves the only sound on the cobblestones, reverberating off the blondestone walls of the dwelling places and the distant echoes returning from the shear faces of the faraway mountains standing steadfast across the plains beyond the City outskirts. He slowed to a canter then to walking pace, needed time to take it all in – the emptiness, the loneliness, the bleakness – it was *wonderful*. His thoughts turned to those who died defending this place over the millennia. The brave warriors who gave up their lives so that haggii could live a life without fear or foreboding – a life that didn't need to consider the invasion of other specie. Until now that is.

He was about to join that noble breed of warrior - would any young Haggis think of him in the centuries to come? Would they think of him kindly? Would they think of him as an Engineer? As a Mercenary? Immortalised in the Haggii Nation's Chronicles? Would there be anyone left? Well, if anyone's to be here the immediate problem needs to be resolved – can keep the thoughts of fighting back marauding invaders for another time. Or is that invading marauders?

He slept that night, first time for ages, although his mind wouldn't slow up or quicken down replaying the worst crash ever – over and over and over. Perfect pain fulfilled, gliding; peacefully, beautifully, tranquilly. 'Life's sweet, being dead'.

Fast-forward – they pulled him back, couldn't let him go, *no-way*, hadn't suffered enough over the years seemingly, and anyhow, only the good die young!

Dawn brought his wits rushing back with a sixty-four thousand volt jolt to the system and rendered his pea-soup senses sensible once again. Already at his workshops when Ben and a delegation from the Wise Council of Haggii Elders arrived. 'Everything still on?' asked Ben. Shug gave a nod without looking up intent on fusing the hypersliders to his knees and shoulders.

'Are you sure there is no other way?' This time Shug did look up. It was the voice of Herod of the Hezmanni. 'Herod, what are you doing here?' croaked Shug.

He scanned the workshop. Not only the entire Council and Herod, but also delegations and faces from the FDR, FEPAC, *and* CSN!

'Well, well, well,' thought Shug, 'a lot of inquisitive creatures here to see this dead haggis walking!' He stopped himself in his tracks – was being cynical and knew there was no need to be – everyone was on his side and had the same problem, they want a solution, they want to leave a world that their young can and will be proud to inherit, have a fighting chance to grow and enjoy what challenges life has to offer. Life - that word takes on a new meaning this morning. Can the tide be turned?

Dani of St Icarus Bay, Nathaniel of Trax, many of the Edenites, and his mum & Janice. A voice from the back shouted 'Nessie sends her love.' It was Smiling Jack Water-Buffalo beaming from ear-to-ear. Calculus Haggis, Big Bill from BerriBerriHill, Angus Haggis, Prebble Haggis, Dr Jon – everyone that was anyone in fact. In the presence of greatness or what?

Spitfire Bob smiled ruefully, Vibex looked on ominously, ArundleSprocketSphere sycophantically standing in their shadow clinging onto their petticoat tails, (metaphorically speaking of course). The Haggettes didn't look any happier, shuffling uneasily in the corner. Annette smiled thinly and tried unconvincingly to sound optimistic with a sheepish 'Hi!' Dr Jon looked as stern as ever, staring into middle distance. Prebble Haggis shuffled forwards stooping as he shook Shug's hand, 'Careful son.'

Ben, with a narrowing of his eyes and a knowing nod confirmed their theorem on quintyllium, halogen, and oxygen. He looked as anxious as alltheothers.

'Christ', thought Shug, 'why are you lot so sad, you shouldn't worry about me, I certainly don't.'

Hamish smiled, quietly oblivious as ever. 'Do you need a hand with anything, Shug?' he whispered in his dulcet tones.

'No, you're alright mate, you know me, on top-of-it always.'

You could cut the atmosphere with a rusty knife.

The sweet smell of heavy gearbox oil and light aquacent-cooling fluid filled the air. 'God', he loved being in his workshops.

'You know there's no other way, Herod; you weren't at the rendezvous with Magdalena or on the banks of Loch Ness with Nessie. This is the only way to produce oxygen in the quantities we need without destroying half the planet.'

'Can someone take your place?'

'Who,' laughed Shug?

It was no laughing matter, and everyone knew it. 'There is no one else quick enough... jeezz, I don't even know if I'm quick enough.' He was becoming carnapsious. Nerves maybe?

'Is it worth it?'

'What?'

'Is *it* worth it?'

'Good timing, Ben, I concede that. What about the needs of the many and all that?'

'We could leave, abandon this world and move to the nearest planet that can support life. Would only take a couple of hundred years.'

'A couple of hundred years?' You know it's at least a thousand years, with almost zero chances of survival for anyone on such a colossal journey. And we're not just talking Haggii here, but the entire animal kingdom!' Shug knew Ben was serious, and also knew that his old friend was terrified of his chances of survival attempting to produce oxygen in this way.

'Of course it's worth it,' said Shug, unconvincingly. 'Can *I* tell a story, just for a change?'

'You remember when I started out I worked in that god-for-saken mine – three thousand feet below ground and four miles to the face line from the bottom of the shaft. The heat and humidity were stifling, you couldn't breathe because of the dust, and on top of that you had eight hours of removing as much coal with a pick as was physically possible – no automation then. Within minutes of starting work you'd be soaking with sweat due to the exertion and, because of the humidity, would be soaking the whole shift. Everyday when I finished and got to the surface, I'd quench my thirst with a bottle of ice cold ginger wine. The stuff I buy now never tastes as good, and do you know why? Toil. I've never had to work as hard as that since – and the sheer effort ensured that the ginger wine was in some kind of way the reward. The reward you get out of anything is directly proportional to the effort you put in. The wine doesn't taste as good now because the effort of working up the thirst is gone.

It's the same with ¾SofL. It's taken me years of blood, sweat, and tears to get this close and I can now attempt it in a great cause too. If I fail your packing up and moving on proposal is acceptable. For everyone left that is.'

Janice walked forward holding Shug's body armour towards him. She was a beautiful fawn; massive heart gentle personality – "Young and sweet and good and kind." Would break many Haggii hearts when she was older, that's for sure. We know how shy she is – getting in the limelight in this company? Maybe she was just worried about Shug.

The bulky armour would slow him. Also, it would have no benefit if he got it wrong at these speeds, couldn't say that to Janice 'though. 'Thanks Janice, get out of here you're stealing my thunder.'

'Mum said I could cook tonight,' she said breathlessly, gasping down air in her excitement.

'What you gonna cremate now, *Janice Haggis?*'

'That's not fair; you know I've been getting better. The steamed thistles last week for instance; they weren't too bad, eh? And what about the poached oysters in porridge and scotch sauce, and the....'

'*Alright, alright*, enough... OK it *was* unfair, so, what wonderfully exotic creation will you be concocting tonight?'

My first ever champion's meal, and you're the true champion, will be...' she paused for effect *and* to get his attention, knew he wasn't listening.

'Sorry, carry on - what you making?'

'You're favourite, fat boy – dah *dah* dah; Vindaloo Escargot! Might not be as good as yours, but will have it ready when you get back from the race. Don't be late.'

She occupied more and more space in his dreams about the future… "and the World's such an unsafe place"… a recurring thought these days, the words torturing his soul as he set off for the collider.

Don't be late?

Late for what?

He knew fine well…

Chapter 30

'You know a mistake is final Ben, don't wait for help, finish it in the collider, finish me – if I'm not already... no one can make it back from spills at these speeds – don't even consider it. Promise me.'

'Promises, promises. The facts of life. What was it you said about the only thing worse than losing your heart's desire...?' his voice tailing off segueing into a gentle sigh.

'Gaining it!' Shug's answer was immaterial, 'and anyway, I was quoting someone else.'

Chapter 31

'Let me get this straight,' said Vibex, 'the entire proposal relies on the exact amount, *by mass,* of quintyllium being reduced to its atomic particles, accelerated along the collider in excess of ¾SofL to annihilate an equal amount of positrons and electrons of halogen, triggering a chain reaction that will produce oxygen on a global scale?'

'Our calculations, Magdalena's, Nessie's, and mine, and not forgetting the work Calculus and Ben had ploughed into this, show the reaction is self-perpetuating, that is, it will go on forever,' offered Shug.

'Is that *soooo*?'

Vibex was never, and has never been receptive to new ideas. Sarcasm became him beautifully. Shug remembered a story that Ben had told him a few years back of the engineer that was once Vibex:-

'Yes, he was an engineer, in the early days of the renaissance he was actually very well respected – his knowledge of soil mechanics was unsurpassed. No one would have thought that the military would win him over quite so convincingly, no one I have ever known has sold out so completely and so absolutely – killed innocent women and children and enjoyed doing so. The quintessential SuperScab!'

Shug remembered thinking at the time, this wasn't like Ben, he had never heard him speak anyone down never heard him speak of anyone in such a deprecating manner – not like him at all. There must be something more between him and Vibex. Surely?

Vibex continued 'as I see it, remembering I wasn't at the meeting between you and Magdalena, there are several non-trivial technical problems that need to be resolved if the plan is to succeed. Firstly, how will the halogen atoms be introduced into the path of the quintyllium? Secondly, nothing had been accelerated beyond ¾ the speed of light anywhere at any time on the entire planet, excepting light, obviously. How is it that we can get quintyllium to outstrip this speed? And thirdly,' pausing for effect, 'the Collider to my knowledge hasn't been used in a million years, does it still work? Do the Edenites still retain the technical skills to make it work?'

'All relevant points,' conceded Shug, 'and all of which I have possible answers to.'

'Possible?'

'Well yes. Possible... probable... feasible... call it what you will. I need a few days to finalise the details we have been working on, dot the i's and cross the t's, and only then, will I have something that we can move on. Proceed. Also, there is a fourth point that you have failed to consider... consider this; if we don't resolve points one, two, *and* three everyone will be dead... is this a *point*

263

worthy of your consideration… Sir?' (This was unusual, usually he could be beaten hands down by the inferior-superior's silver tongue, it usually took him a good ten minutes after the debate to come up with a convincing answer, a true answer, - this was it, an instantaneous answer to the underhanded fool's mind-numbing question; yessss)!

Shug was being flippant and argumentative and knew he would get no support with this tack – what was the saying?, "a speech made in anger is the best speech your ever likely to regret!" He continued trying a softer approach, 'hey, think of it this way – the reaction is self-perpetuating that's the simplest of simple beauty. In the accelerator electrons collide with positrons at ¾SofL they annihilate each other in an eruption of pure energy from which arises new elementary particles – mother nature couldn't achieve it better herself. You have to believe me… us, it's the only way.'

Chapter 32

Shug climbed into the collider to complete several shakedown circuits to permit the Edenites to calibrate their instrumentation and dial in their telemetry to ensure the conditions would be optimised so that the reaction had the best possible chance of crystallizing. Also, it would let Ben test his newly designed barrier layers & rhythm shifters to give him as much protection as possible and the best chance of survival. The walls, floor, and roof of the inside of the collider merged into one smooth surface of a metal alloy way beyond anything anyone on this world had ever imagined or created – the ultimate in alchemistic wizardry. He had to attain the magic speed of 140,000 miles per second if the reaction was to be born.

The first run was disastrous, barely going supersonic. The floor of the structure was super smooth and didn't give him enough grip to get the purchase he needed to drive forwards. Emerging from the collider with the solemn faces of Ben, Calculus and the Edenites looking at him wondering 'what's the matter with you?' 'Don't worry people I just need to make a small modification to my boots – do you have a machine shop?'.

'Of course,' answered Daniel, ' sure – anything you need'

'Thanks, just show me where it is and leave me for an hour to get this sorted.'

Shug entered the machine shop and bolted his boots to the bed of a five axis milling machine. Some quick programming later and he was ready to start cutting metal. The idea was to cut fine criss-cross curvilinear grooves into the souls that would bite into the collider to help him propel himself forward.

Just under an hour later, he had refitted the boots and was climbing back into the 'arena'. 'OK gentlehaggii, *one... more... time...*'

'Shug, another small problem you should know about before you have your second run,' said Ben as he was about to lock down the hatch. 'The sonic boom which occurred earlier when you broke the sound barrier nearly shook the structure to pieces, something the Edenites hadn't considered in the construction, meaning we are limited on the number of practice runs you can make.'

'Brilliant!'

'It isn't really an issue as, on the vinegar run, we'll have pulled the collider down to vacuum so sonic disturbances won't be an issue,' Ben explained trying to be supportive.

The "vinegar run"? This was a slang term the Haggii used meaning ultimate, or definitive, or final – it meant "do or die".

So, with that, they closed the hatch and Ben activated the relevant mechanisms to ensure an airtight and explosion proof seal.

The mod's to the boots worked better than anyone had hoped for and by the end of the first lap of the next practice run, according to his bio-speedometer, he was travelling at 100,000 miles per second. Disaster though, was about to strike. As he slowed down and dropped below the speed of sound, the sonic boom he had created caught up with him and in a massive burst of energy threw him like a rag doll down the collider for several miles, before coming to a stop in a crumpled mess of torn flesh and crushed body armour. Within seconds several hatches in close vicinity to where he was lying cracked open and Edenites clambered in and begun attending to the injuries.

It was terrible.

Back in the control room, Ben and the others listened intently to the radio discussions that were taking place between the distraught medics at the scene and the doctors in the medical lab. The damage wasn't as bad as first envisaged, but full body and neuro scans were required to confirm this. They removed him from the collider and transported him to the medical centre, where Ben and Calculus were already waiting. When he got there, Shug had regained consciousness and was attempting to explain to the medics everything was fine. He didn't look fine. Ben convinced him to let them go through their checks, get him through the various scanners, and then they could take a view as how best to proceed.

For everyone concerned, to a soul, it was the longest night of their life.

They patched him up as best they could and he returned to the control room to see what the instrumentation had picked up before he 'stepped-off'. Luckily, the poison from the envenomation process was still in his system and prevented catastrophic damage to his fragile skeletal structure and on-the-edge central nervous system.

The Edenite telemetry confirmed what his bio-speedometer had indicated that indeed the speed achieved was in excess of 100,000 miles per second, but it also showed that he was close to passing the midway section of the outside wall, that is, pushed any further he would be running above the midway height which, if passed then the strength required to get past ¾SofL would be significantly greater. He had to concentrate on being below this meridian. The biosensors they had fitted showed his heart-rate, breathing, and blood pressure, were well within acceptable limits. Unsurprisingly, they didn't discuss his neuron activity. It didn't bother him, at this stage his mind had to be reacting quicker than it had ever done before.

The structure was still intact, but the advice was that any subsequent runs should be under vacuum as they couldn't guarantee that another sonic pressure wave similar to the one that had occurred the previous evening wouldn't result in catastrophic failure of the collider superstructure.

Shug and Ben and Calculus retired to an antechamber to discuss their limited options. 'Do you think you can do it?' was the opener from Calculus, closely followed by 'Is it safe?' from Ben.

'Yes and no,' replied Shug.

'Meaning you think you can do it, and that it isn't safe?' said Ben

'Yup.'

'Shall we call it off?'

'No way! I haven't gone through all this to fall at the final hurdle. Everything's working isn't it – the vacuum pumps, the induction heaters, the halogen injectors? Yes? Even your barrier layers and rhythm shifters, Ben?'

'It's up to you - no one will blame you if you pull out now.'

'Who said anything about pulling out? I'm ready if you and the Edenites are. I don't need another test run, I'm ready to go for it for real. Remember, it's my funeral.'

'Don't tempt fate young haggis!'

They returned to the control room and Ben gave the Edenite technicians the instruction to go; 'we're on, people.'

A momentary pause and universal look of disbelief swept over their faces... and then it was all hands to the pumps and the countdown was underway.

Shug climbed back into the collider and started warming up as the sound of the massive vacuum pumps kicked in and the collider's oxygen started to be evacuated.

The clock was ticking.

Timing was everything – start too soon and the atmospheric conditions wouldn't be right – temperature, pressure, catalyst volume and mass, but on the other hand, start too late and there wouldn't be enough time for the rhythm shifters and barrier layers to protect him from the climatic conditions that would kill him.

It was intense.

In the control room Calculus was close to throwing up, or as Daniel liked to call it - "swallowing out". 'What's the matter with you?' enquired Ben.

'What? How can you be calm at a time like this?'

'Don't worry my old learned friend, Shug's on it!'

The Edenites were still making last minute checks and adjustments, hundreds upon hundreds of dials, gauges, sensors, and graphs being checked and rechecked as the countdown beacon turned to green and the ten-second pulse begun. Shug would feel this as punchy electric shocks from the sensors on his chest.

….three….two….one…..zero!

Ben and Calculus looked at each other in silent terror, both thinking 'the day I've dreaded all my life has arrived.'

Shug had already passed the 100K mark and was pulling strong as he headed towards the elusive ¾SofL.

The spotlights that were placed every 816yards in the roof of the collider became a single beam and got dimmer and dimmer and dimmer as he got faster and faster and faster. He could feel the rhythm shifter stopping and starting his heart, knowing that soon, the pressure form the barrier layers, as they kicked in, would hit him in the back like a mighty sledgehammer – this wouldn't happen until ¾SofL and the reaction would be happening, if all went well. He could 'though, surprisingly enough, smell the pungent stench of halogen. It made his eyes sting.

As 140,000 miles per second was approached there was a blinding flash, a blinding white light hit him full in the face like an express train, he stopped running, everything went silent – no rush, no burning, no halogen, no pressure kicks. His heart returned to normal – no rhythm shifting. Now the light wasn't in front, or behind for that matter – but everywhere, and nowhere – he couldn't pin point the origin or where it was emanating from. Strange.

'I've failed. It hasn't worked. We were all wrong – our experiments, our calculations; Magdalena, Nessie, the Sages – we

271

were all wrong! I was wrong. How can it be? *How can that be?'*
Suddenly, Ben was at his shoulder, he was still moving after all,
and moving very very quickly indeed.

'Well?'

'What the…?!!?'

'You've done it! The reaction is happening and you've left the
collider. Nothing to worry about now. You've saved the planet.
Already the news has spread worldwide and the armies are being
disassembled, the catapults dismantled, miners packing up,
everyone returning to their respective Nation. You did it. Can you
believe it? Well done!'

'I don't understand, what's going on?'

'You do understand, it's very simple; you arrived at the
collider, applied what you have learned, and left to be delivered
here. Everyone is saved, life will go on, maybe not as blissfully
and free of pain and suffering as we would like, but it *will* go on.'

'Deliverance? I still don't understand! You need to be more
specific, less CRYPTIC!'

'Life will go on and the Nations of the planet will grow and
learn, and in time maybe learn to live together, at least until the
next time "extinction lurks". You said it, remember?'

'If I'm not in the collider, where am I then?'

'You're with me… we're on the other side.'

'Start making sense, will you?'

'Simple. ¾SofL is the key, it defines life. It's not about speed it's about belief – belief in yourself, belief in your people, belief in life. You would never get to this speed by pure physical prowess and mental dexterity alone, you need to believe in yourself and when you do everything changes, nothing will be the same again, ever.'

'Tell me you're not talking about transcendence, tell me you're not.'

'That's exactly what I'm telling you, but it's not quite what the religious tyrants think it is, nothing like that at all. If you stay you'll learn this.'

'If I stay?'

They fell silent for a while still travelling beyond ¾SofL, somewhere in the ether, some where in the heavens. Whilst, at the same time Shug felt they were stationary, above themselves looking down on themselves. It was the strangest sensation ever. He wasn't sure he liked it. Ben broke the silence.

'You can reject the offer if you like. Go back to the Nation, back to Haggii City Central, take back your mortal coil, live with the Haggii, get married, have fawns, grow old, there's nothing wrong with that, many great haggii, some of the greatest haggii have chosen that vocation. But understand, you have been chosen, you did not choose, you turn your back on this now, and it is unlikely to happen to you again.'

'So what's your story then? Are you an immortal that walks among us mere mortals?'

Ben deftly deflected the question, 'I can take you back to the collider if you like, but can't guarantee you will emerge from it alive, can't guarantee you'll survive the reaction.'

Shug focused, his mind was as rapid as it had ever been, he wasn't going to be bamboozled by enigmatic wholehearted advice, 'there's too much still to do Ben, too much danger for the Nation; Vibex, the Oraxonites, the Icaria. King Bob and the humans can't be trusted. I don't know what I can do for the Haggii and the fawns when I'm within the Nation, but if I'm here I know I can't do anything, I can't influence anything; they'll be on their own. So helpless, so vulnerable.'

'I'm not permitted to advise you or direct you on this, so the choice is yours. What will *you* do? But before deciding, think of this; to walk with the immortals is to walk with greatness, to walk and to shape everything, you can do great work throughout the Universe, forever, and there are many specie the length and breadth of the void that are in as much danger as the threat you defeated today. Let me show you.'

They were transported to various places and times in the universe, Ben wanting to show him the pain and suffering that so many millions faced. Shug thought quietly of the words coming from a very different being to the being he knew as Benjamin

Augustus Haggis. But in a way, deep down, he had always known Ben was a bit special; and with that the decision was made....

'Take me back! Let me go back.'

After the numbness and disorientation the first sensation he felt was the rhythm shifter kicking back in and his heart stopping, starting, and quivering, like the ignition on an internal combustion engine being advanced and retarded. Then the massive hammer blows on his back as the barrier layers energised between him and the ferocious reactions taking place behind. The faster he went the further out the rhythm shifter threw his heart beat and the more fierce and syncopated the hammer blows became, until whoosh he was down; tumbling, head over heels, end over end over end. It went on for an age, until everything stopped, everything became very silent, anechoic. Couldn't move, dared not move.

He slipped into unconsciousness and then into death.

Chapter 33

The barrier layers held well against the brutal generation and production of oxygen that was taking place on the opposite side of the field to where Shug lay prostrate.

Motionless.

Hatches cracked open and Edenites poured into the now ice cold collider. They had to get him out as quickly as possible as the field that formed the barrier layer was breaking down, draining the entire facility of energy.

They rushed him to the only state-of-the-art clinic that could bring him back. He went through a twenty-four hour operation still dead, the only thing keeping him from becoming a vegetable were the gallons of synthetic blood and oxygen being pumped through his stagnant brain. His heart wouldn't react to any external stimuli so was being mechanically compressed and expanded by a mechanical 'hand' inserted into his chest cavity. All of his other major organs had failed and science and the scientists were undertaking the work they would usually do as a matter of course. Most of the Doctors thought the procedure was futile but Benjamin Augustus Haggis wouldn't let them give up. Even his mum and Janice thought it beyond hope.

Dani of the Icaria arrived and whispered a few words to Ben that agitated him more than a little. Shug's clothes and armour were strewn on the operating room floor, Ben began furiously checking through the pockets, pouches, and compartments of the garments, finding nothing and dropping to his knees shouting 'Nooooo....!'

'Are these what you're looking for?' Ben looked up to see Dr Jon standing with outstretched palms, in one the serpent's head and in the other the serpent's rattler both of which Shug had cut off in the Icarian cave. 'I can't let you use these, it's against everything we stand for, and you know the non-negotiable price that has to be paid.'

'It's different,' said Ben, 'you have to trust me on this; you don't know what I know. We have exhausted all avenues to resuscitate him, if Shug doesn't have these we should turn off the machines now. Is that what you want?'

'Tell me more, I can't consider this course of action if you don't tell me what the get-out clause that you're eluding to is – and that's what you're doing, isn't it?'

'There's no get-out clause, you know who we're dealing with, you know that. You just have to trust me... please?'

Jon reluctantly handed the head and rattler over, but as Ben stretched out his hand to take them, Jon wouldn't let go until he had a long stare into Ben's eyes and soul – with a clear message; 'don't mess this up!'

Ben called for Dani to be brought back into the operating theatre. 'Here do what you need to do, HURRY!'

Dani began grinding the serpent's head and rattler to dust, then in the same receptacle added a fluid from a vessel she conjured from nowhere. Using a syringe bigger than any of them had ever seen, she stabbed Shug in the neck, plunging the needle right to the hilt before injecting the fluid.

Within seconds, all of the equipment attached to Shug began to come alive - bleeping, whirring, flashing, everything lit up and then settled down into weak signs of vital organs beginning to work for themselves. It was wonderful, if maybe, a bit premature.

'It will be sometime before we can be sure,' said Dani as she hurried out of the operating room, out of the clinic, and back to the mountains over St Icarus Bay.

'YOU! You had better know what you're doing,' said Dr Jon as he too hurried out of the clinic.

Ben stood silent and motionless for some time, before addressing Janice and Shug's mum – 'come, it will be sometime before we will know, there's nothing else we can do here.'

They left the Doctors and Scientists to prepare Shug for the coma that lay ahead. After some hours, they powered down all the machines and equipment that had been keeping him alive, fitted a drip to his arm which would keep his nutrition levels stable, monitors to his heart and brain to check progress, turned off the lights and locked the door behind them, leaving him alone for the long anxious nightmare that was about to be endured.

Chapter 34

Five long years passed.

Shug's mum was sitting in her kitchen with her head in her hands when suddenly Janice barged in 'quick, quick the Doctors want to see us, quick!' They both rushed from the house up to the clinic. Running down corridors to Shug's room they came across everyone; Dr Jon, BAH, Big Bill, Herod. 'What is it, what's going on?'

Everyone looked at Dr Jon. Shug's mum repeated the question, and Jon finally answered. 'Shug's awake but still nowhere near can he be considered recovered, but things *are* looking good.'

'Can we see him?'

'Yes, come this way.'

They entered the room and the haggis in the bed in front of them was a very different haggis to the son and brother they had known, but immediately knew he was with them, was here, was still alive. Eyes open and receptive. They were overjoyed. They were overcome.

After a while Janice took his mum home to rest in a dark room and be relieved that a recovery was possible.

The others stayed with him for a couple of hours before drifting off alone or in pairs, until Big Bill from BerriBerri Hill was left alone with Dr Jon.

'So?'

Jon shrugged his shoulders and held his palms skywards.

'*SO*? What's happened to Shug? Will he recover?' Bill wasn't an elephant that needed rhetoric, he liked creatures to shoot from the hip.

Jon for once wasn't his usual bombastic self and became simultaneously solemn, humble, *and,* profound.

For the record, this is what he said –

'That young haggis is long gone and the shell you see before you is all that's left. In time, the tortured soul and broken body will heal, the nightmares will cease and the dreams shall return. In spite of it all there is more depth and greater wisdom in the being that's left and what's 'misplaced' *will* be found; in the end salvation lies within. But for now, his mind and his soul will go about their secret business of assembling a testimony of truth and finding contrasts and parallels in everything that has come to pass. They can't help it and he can't stop it.'

To sleep… per chance to dream.

About the Author

Steve Cooper was born in 1962 on St Andrew's day in Glasgow.

After working as a fitter at the Face in dank Scottish Collieries through the 80s, he continued his Engineering studies at Strathclyde University followed by a Business Degree at the University of Glasgow before moving to Australia in 2008.

Steve lives in the leafy suburbs of Melbourne with his partner Lynnie.

He is a professional engineer, amateur motorcycle racer, and perpetual garage-band drummer.

When not writing, his favourite pastimes are travelling, cooking, and sharing a cold beer and champagne with family and friends.